ANNE MATHER

living with adam

HARLEQUIN BOOKS
toronto-winnipeg

CHAPTER ONE

DR. ADAM MASSEY brought his car to a halt outside the tall, narrow Georgian façade of the fashionable Chelsea town house that Loren liked to call her *pied-à-terre*. Looking thoughtfully up at the windows, Adam wondered how she would take the news he had to impart, and knew without a shadow of a doubt that she would not like it. But then he didn't particularly care for the idea himself.

He compressed his lips wryly and turning off the engine he put the ignition keys into his pocket. As he slid almost reluctantly out of the car he was conscious that he was simply delaying the inevitable, and with an impatient shrug of his broad shoulders he locked the car door and, turning, ran swiftly up the stone steps of the house. Inserting his key in the lock, he entered the softly carpeted hallway, and encountered Alice, Loren's invaluable maidservant who had been with her for more years than she cared to remember. Alice smiled, and said:

'Oh, it's you, doctor. I thought it was another of those reporters! Cheek of the devil they have.'

Adam frowned and glanced at his watch. 'Damn,' he exclaimed. 'I'd forgotten. It was the press conference this afternoon, wasn't it? Are Mannering and Edwards still here?'

'Mr. Mannering's gone, but Mr. Edwards is still here,' Alice informed him. 'It's almost finished, anyway. I'm sure Miss Griffiths would be only too pleased to send them away if she knew you were here.'

Adam gave a rather dry smile. 'You're very good for my ego, Alice,' he said, with feeling. 'However, I really don't think I ought to interrupt her while she's working—'

'*Darling!*'

The voice came from above, drifting down to them huskily, and both Adam and the housekeeper looked up to see Loren Griffiths poised at the head of the flight of stairs which led down into the hall. Dressed in a clinging gown of some dusky pink material that clung to her small, supple form, her blonde hair swinging silkily to her shoulders, she was quite startlingly beautiful, and Adam thrust his hands patiently into his trousers pockets, quite aware that Loren was about to make an entrance. She came down the stairs with her usual elegance, but there was a certain eagerness in her step which quickened as she neared him and presently she was sliding both her arms possessively about one of his.

'Darling,' she said again, 'you know perfectly well I hate these conferences, but they're a necessary evil, I'm afraid!'

Adam half smiled. 'You know you revel in every minute of it,' he contradicted her gently. 'What's happened? Where are your avid critics?'

Loren raised her dark eyebrows. 'If you mean the press, and I presume you do when you speak in that sarcastic tone, they're all having drinks with Terry.'

Terry Edwards was her agent, and Adam suppressed the ready comment he could have made. He and Edwards just didn't get on, and it was no secret.

'I see,' he said, instead. 'I was just remarking to Alice that I had forgotten you would be busy this afternoon. However, if you're through . . .'

6

'I am. But, darling, I thought it was your baby clinic this afternoon, or something.' She wrinkled her nose delicately, and Alice chose this moment to say:

'Shall I bring you something to the small sitting-room, Miss Griffiths?'

'Just tea, please, Alice,' said Adam before Loren could reply, and Alice nodded agreeably and disappeared in the direction of the kitchen.

Loren sighed rather petulantly and then said: 'Really, Adam, you might consult me before issuing Alice with your orders!'

Adam smiled. 'Don't fuss. Come into the sitting-room. I want to talk to you.'

'Only talk? You disappoint me,' returned Loren dryly, but she preceded him obediently across the hall and into the small sitting-room which was the least opulently furnished room in the house. Even so, its tapestry-clad walls and Regency-striped couches set on soft Aubusson carpeting were a little stifling for Adam's taste, but he usually managed to hide his feelings admirably.

Now Loren waited until he had closed the door before twining her arms round his neck and parting his lips with her own, pressing her lissom body close against him, demanding a response. Adam held her closely for a moment, returning her kiss warmly, and then he gently but firmly put her away from him. When she would have protested and slid back into his arms, his grip on her arms tightened perceptibly, and she pouted impatiently.

'Adam,' she said reproachfully, 'I thought you'd come here to see me.'

Adam sighed. 'So I did, Loren. But not for the reasons you imagine. I have other things on my mind

7.

right now.'

Loren pulled out of his grasp. 'Oh, have you?'

'I'm afraid so.' Adam raked a hand through his thick dark hair which persisted in falling across his forehead. 'I'm sorry, Loren, but I'm not in the mood to play games!'

Loren compressed her lips. 'You're a cool devil, Adam,' she exclaimed angrily. 'You come here unexpected and unannounced, and then when I try to show you how pleased I am to see you, you treat it all like child's play!' She tossed her head. 'I don't know why I put up with it!'

Adam's eyes narrowed. 'Why do you?' His tone was hard.

Loren looked at him impatiently, and then she gave a helpless gesture of submission. 'Oh, Adam, don't let's quarrel! You know I don't mean half of what I say. It's just that I get so – so jealous – of your time – of everything.'

Adam's face softened. 'All right, Loren, we won't quarrel. I just don't know how to put what I have to say.'

Loren went and sat on a couch and patted the seat beside her invitingly, but Adam shook his head and paced rather restlessly about the room until Alice appeared with a tray of tea and some hot buttered scones which she placed on a low table in front of Loren. She smiled rather understandingly at him before leaving, and after she had gone, Loren picked up the teapot rather carelessly and began to pour some tea into the wafer-thin cups.

'What is it about you that makes women feel so protective towards you?' she asked tersely. 'Honestly, Alice treats you like a long-lost son, and although she knows I

8

hate tea she persists in making it because you're here!' She made a moue with her lips. 'You don't look in need of protection to me!'

Adam smiled and came to take the cup she held out for him. 'Don't be bitter!' he commented mockingly, and she lifted her shoulders with some annoyance before squeezing lemon into her own tea and grimacing as she raised the cup to her lips.

'Well, anyway,' she went on, after taking several sips of the liquid, 'why are you here? I'm sure you said it was your baby clinic this afternoon.'

'It was.' Adam bent and put one of the tiny scones into his mouth. 'But Hadley is taking it for me.'

'But why? You know we had a date for dinner after the play this evening. Can't you make that?' There was a taut resigned expression marring her perfect features now.

Adam shrugged. 'Emergencies aside, I can't see why not,' he replied smoothly. 'But what I have to tell you seemed better said when you're fresh, and not when you're tired after the play, as you invariably are.'

Loren frowned. 'You make me sound like a creaking Madonna!' she exclaimed. 'I'm never too tired for you.'

He inclined his head slowly. 'All right, perhaps I used the wrong expression. In any event, I wanted to talk to you now, while we're alone, and not in some crowded restaurant.'

'Well, do go on. I'm avid to hear what it is.'

Adam sighed, and replaced his tea cup on its saucer. 'Well,' he began carefully, 'my mother has written to ask me to look after Maria for six months.'

There was silence for a long moment, and then Loren said, slowly: 'Who is Maria?'

9

Adam shrugged his broad shoulders. 'My stepsister. I've mentioned her.'

Loren's nostrils flared slightly. 'Your stepsister,' she repeated tautly.

'Yes.'

Loren rose to her feet, reaching for a cigarette from the box on the table and accepting the light Adam offered. Inhaling deeply, she looked intently at him. 'Perhaps I'm slightly dense, Adam, but why have you to look after your stepsister for six months? I thought you told me she was practically grown-up?'

'She is. At least, she must be. It's five years since I last saw her. She was twelve or thirteen then, I'm not certain which.'

Loren was obviously controlling her temper with difficulty as she asked: 'But your stepsister lives with your mother and her father in Ireland. Exactly why are you involved?'

Adam thrust his hands into his pockets. 'She wants to come to London to take a secretarial course.'

'A secretarial course?' echoed Loren faintly. 'Why can't she take this course in Dublin or somewhere?' Her eyes flashed with impatience.

Adam raised his eyebrows. 'Your guess is as good as mine.'

'But it's ludicrous!' Loren shook her head disbelievingly. 'Saddling you with a teenage girl! What is your mother thinking of?' Her eyes narrowed suddenly. 'She knows about – me – doesn't she?'

'My mother? Of course.'

Loren nodded her head vigorously. 'I thought so. That's it, of course.'

Adam sighed. 'What is "it"?'

'She's sending this girl here to spy upon us.'

'Oh, don't be ridiculous!' Adam raked a hand through his hair. 'I'm not a child, Loren. I am over thirty, you know.'

'I know, darling, but until your mother married again, you were her little ewe-lamb, weren't you?'

'Loren, don't talk such tripe! If she's sending Maria to London, it must be because Maria wants to come.'

'But why should she want to come?'

'How the hell should I know?' Adam strode across to the window. 'What would you have me say? I'm sorry, but she can't come. My – my mistress would object?'

Loren uttered a furious gasp. 'You – you—'

'Oh, save it!' exclaimed Adam, turning round. 'I'm sorry, I shouldn't have said that. Nevertheless, it's true. She is my stepsister, after all, and I don't see much of her. As I recall she was a nice kid. At least she didn't throw any tantrums when her father married my mother, and I know my mother found it easier because of her understanding. Girls of ten can be pretty difficult at times.'

Loren's lips thinned. 'And exactly where is she to live?'

Adam frowned. 'At the house, I guess.'

'At your house? In Kensington?'

'I guess so, why?'

'Isn't that a little unorthodox?'

'In this day and age! You must be joking?'

'Nevertheless, you are – a – bachelor, you live alone—'

'I have Mrs. Lacey. She lives in.'

'A housekeeper!' Loren's voice was scornful.

Adam regarded her broodingly. 'All right then, marry me and provide a chaperon!'

Loren looked at him impatiently. 'What? And live in

that urban backwater? No, thank you, Adam.' She drew deeply on her cigarette.

Adam shrugged and after regarding her for several minutes more, walked swiftly towards the door.

'No! Wait!' Loren gathered herself and ran after him, grasping his arm and dragging him round to look at her. 'I'm sorry, Adam, I'm sorry. That was a terrible way to put it. But honestly, we've had this out before, I just couldn't go on like that!'

'I know.' Adam's features were taut.

'But it's so unnecessary anyway,' she cried. 'You know Matthew Harding would be overjoyed if you joined his staff!'

Adam's face became sardonic. 'I've told you before, Loren, I don't practise that kind of medicine!'

'How many kinds are there?' she protested.

He lifted his shoulders rather wearily. 'I prefer my kind,' he replied dryly.

'You prefer visiting that ghastly East End clinic to me, I suppose!' Loren bit furiously at her lips.

'You know that's not true,' he returned quietly, 'nevertheless, I will not give up my work – even for you. And nor will I join some plushy West End practitioner who spends his time dispensing psychology to over-fed, over-indulged, and over-anxious hypochondriacs!'

Loren thrust herself away from him. 'Being ill isn't the prerogative of the poor, you know,' she said bitterly.

Adam regarded her sombrely. 'No, I agree,' he said calmly. 'I suppose I meet just as many hypochondriacs in my work as anyone else. However, the percentage of my patients who feign illness has to be less when I consider how many patients I see a day compared to old Harding.'

'Mr. Harding is a friend of mine.'

'I know that.'

'He thinks he's a friend of yours, too.'

'Did I say he wasn't?'

'No, but – oh, you're impossible.' Loren heaved a sigh. 'Why couldn't you be like everybody else? Why couldn't you put yourself out for me, just for once? You know I love you, you know I want to marry you—'

'But only on your terms, is that it?' Adam opened the door. 'I must go. I've got to go to St. Michael's before evening surgery.'

'Why?' Loren was curious in spite of herself.

'There's a patient there I've got to see.' Adam was cool now.

'A woman?' Loren's tone was guarded.

'Yes.'

Loren tensed. 'Is she more important to you than I am?'

'Right now – yes.'

'Sometimes I hate you, Adam Massey!'

'I'm sorry about that.' Adam gave her a slight smile before going out of the door.

'Adam – wait—' Again she flung herself across the room after him, only to find him in the hall talking to Alice. Alice was saying: 'Did you find out how Mrs. Ainsley was?' and Adam was nodding and telling her that she had had her operation but that she was still very weak.

'I'm going to see her now, actually,' he said. 'She has no one else.'

Alice smoothed her apron. 'Do you think she would like me – I mean—'

'I'm sure she would.' Adam's voice was gentle, and

Loren compressed her lips, a sick feeling rising in her throat. She wanted him so much in that moment, and she knew he was completely indifferent to her right now. Assuming a casual tone, she said, mostly to Alice: 'Who's this you're talking about?'

Alice turned to her. 'Old Mrs. Ainsley,' she replied, frowning. 'You know – I told you – she fell down the stairs a few days ago and injured herself internally.'

'Oh!' Loren's lips formed a surprised circle. Then she looked at Adam. His gaze was coolly sardonic, and she cursed herself for her jealousy. Then she said quickly: 'I – I will see you tonight, won't I, Adam?'

Adam lifted his shoulders. 'I suppose so,' he replied emotionlessly. Then they heard sounds from above and presently several men appeared at the top of the stairs and began coming down, talking and laughing amongst themselves. Adam gave Loren a wry glance, and then said: 'I've got to go. See you later. I'll tell Mrs. Ainsley you might call, shall I, Alice?'

Alice nodded, and accompanied him to the door while Loren was forced to go and meet the members of the press who were about to take their leave. She looked appealingly after Adam, but he did not look back, and with determination she raised a smile and tried to forget the frustration that was tearing her apart.

Outside, Adam slid into his car, not without some relief. Sometimes he wished he had never become involved with Loren Griffiths, but mostly he acknowledged that he enjoyed their association. It was only at times like this when she taunted him about his practice that he realized how differently they viewed life. Fate had chosen that their paths should cross, but, continuing in its pattern, had separated them again. He still recalled with clarity the day her sleek Bentley had collided with his rather practical Rover, and of how apologetic she had been in her attempts to charm and tantalize him out of his reasonable annoyance. She had been at fault, of course, but he was only human after all, and Loren Griffiths was already a household name to theatregoers. He supposed he had been flattered at her attentions, unaware of his own attraction which lay not in the lean strength of his body, or in the rather harsh lines of his face, but rather in the disturbing depths of his eyes which were so dark a grey as to appear black in some lights. In any event, Loren found him extremely attractive, and his brusque manner was at once a change and a pleasure after constant adulation. She had never known a doctor before, at least not a young one, and his lack of deference was refreshing. In no time she had wanted to further his career, seeing herself as Loren Griffiths, the actress, wife of Adam Massey, the famous Harley Street specialist. But unfortunately she had reckoned without Adam's strength of will, and all her attempts to change him had failed abysmally. He was a realist, and he wanted to use his knowledge where it was most needed, not in the furtherance of his own ambitions, but in helping people whom he considered deserved a better deal from life.

Now he heaved a sigh and set the car in motion. As well as visiting Mrs. Ainsley, he had other wheels to set rolling, for although he had not mentioned it to Loren while she was so angry, his mother had really left him little choice in the matter of Maria. He knew, of course, that there might be some truth in what Loren had said regarding his mother's reactions to their relationship. His mother disliked such an association and considered that her son deserved someone more suited to the position of doctor's wife than an actress who in her estimation relied as much on her looks as on her talent. But since her marriage to Patrick Sheridan she had had little opportunity to use her influence with her son. And as Patrick's home was in southern Ireland, she visited London only rarely. Her greatest disappointment, Adam knew, was that he did not visit Kilcarney more often. As he had told Loren, it was five years since he had visited his stepfather's house, and although his mother had visited London two or three times since she had been alone and unable to stay for more than a few days. Her new husband was a farmer, and owned a large spread some miles from Limerick, and consequently he was seldom able to leave it. Adam smiled as he recalled how different his mother's life was now from when she had been married to his father, who had owned a garage in Richmond. He thought she had settled down to life in Ireland very well, but eight years ago when she had told him she was accepting Patrick's proposal, Adam had been immersed in his medical studies and consequently he had not taken the trouble to get to know his stepfather's family particularly well. So long as his mother was happy, which she obviously was, he had been content, and only now did he wonder whether this was her way of attempting to re-establish a relationship with him. Even so, her letter had been unexpected, and he was still unsure as to how to answer it. He supposed he could refuse outright, but what excuse could he offer? His mother knew Mrs. Lacey and trusted her implicitly, so he could not use his bachelor status as a reason for not accepting a teenage girl into his household. And in any case, it was only for six months, which would soon pass, and perhaps Maria herself might tire of the course long before that time was up.

He tried to remember what he knew of her, but five years ago when he had visited Kilcarney he had been newly qualified while she had been a schoolgirl with a rather chunky ponytail and little else to commend her that he could recall.

He drove to St. Michael's Hospital which was situated in a close just off the Embankment. Its stark grey walls revealed its age though its tiled corridors and wards were brightly lit and cheerful. There was talk of its being pulled down and new premises being built, but somehow it continued to survive, and its staff were loyal as well as efficient. Adam had once had the chance of taking a job as houseman here, but he preferred the involvement of general practice.

Mrs. Ainsley was still in a side ward, but her pale cheeks warmed a little as she saw who her visitor was. Living alone as she did her only contact was with the doctor, and Adam knew that she regarded him more as a friend than anything else. Now he sat down on the side of her bed and listened patiently as she described in detail everything that had happened to her since she had been brought to the hospital, and of how friendly everyone had been. Adam thought it was easy to be friendly to someone like Mrs. Ainsley, and felt his usual regret that her only child, a daughter, should have emigrated to Australia several years ago and never seemed to imagine that her mother might require something more than occasional letters from her. The old lady seemed starved of human contact, and although there were societies or clubs she might have joined, she was reticent and retiring, spending her days knitting or sewing, and looking after Minstrel, her elderly spaniel.

When Adam left the hospital, he drove straight to his house in Kensington. Although his practice was in Islington he had continued to live in the house his mother had acquired soon after his father died, for he knew she liked to come back there sometimes. It was not a large house, it had only four bedrooms, but it had the advantage of being detached, and stood inside a small walled garden where it was still pleasant to sit on hot summer evenings. Of course, all about there was evidence of the continual building programme, sky-scraper apartments and office blocks encroaching to the ends of these quiet cul-de-sacs, but the park was not far away and from Adam's upper windows he could see across the expanse of green lawns to the flower gardens.

Now he drove between the stone posts guarding the drive and brought his car to a halt to the side of the house where rhododendrons brushed the bonnet, bur-geoning with spring colour. Sliding out of the car, he walked round the bonnet to the front porch and en-tered into the panelled hall. He was feeling pleasantly thoughtful, and was looking forward to taking a bath before evening surgery. But even as he closed the front door his eyes were attracted to a brilliant orange anorak that was draped over the banister at the foot of the stairs. And as his eyes travelled further he saw also two suitcases, standing side by side below the anorak.

A feeling of impatience gripped him as several thoughts ran through his mind, and he strode swiftly down the hall to the kitchen from where the murmur of voices could be heard. He flung open the door, startling his housekeeper, Mrs. Lacey, who came to greet him excitedly, gesturing at the girl who was perched on one of the tall stools by the breakfast bar.

'You've got a visitor, Mr. Adam,' she said, clasping her hands together agitatedly. 'An unexpected visitor!'

Adam's eyes moved from Mrs. Lacey's animated face to that of the girl who was sliding off the stool as his housekeeper spoke, looking towards them with anticipation, and an expression of irritability crossed his lean face. Despite the fact that her chestnut hair was now trimmed to shoulder length, and her tall young body was slimmer than he remembered, those amber eyes trimmed with dark lashes were the same, as was the generous width of her mouth and the capricious tilt of her nose. And because he recognized her, he felt a rising sense of resentment that his mother should have dared to allow her to come here uninvited.

'Hello, Maria,' he said formally, without any warmth in his voice, but the girl didn't seem at all abashed by his coolness. Instead, her eyes sparkled and she ran across the space between them, winding her arms about his neck and kissing him with enthusiasm on his cheek. Adam was flabbergasted, putting up his hands to catch her wrists and press her away from him, while his startled gaze caught Mrs. Lacey's undisguised amusement. But Maria merely stepped backwards, allowing him momentarily to retain his involuntary hold on her wrists, and smiling mischievously, said: 'Don't look so disapproving, Adam! Aren't you pleased to see me?' Her voice was soft and husky, with a faint brogue that was attractive.

Adam stared at her for a moment, unable to find words to express his feelings, and then he raked a hand through his hair and said: 'How the hell did you get here?'

Maria shrugged her slim shoulders. 'By plane, of course.' She glanced smilingly towards Mrs. Lacey. 'Your housekeeper has been very kind. I arrived about an hour ago.'

Adam heaved a sigh. 'It was only this morning I received my mother's letter asking whether you might be allowed to come here,' he exclaimed sharply. 'I don't know why she bothered to write – in the circumstances.'

Maria's eyes twinkled. 'Oh, but I do, Adam. You see, she doesn't know I've come.'

'What!' Adam was aghast.

Maria raised her dark eyebrows and spread her hands in an eloquent gesture. 'But don't you see, Adam, this is why I came! I felt sure that given time to consider the situation you wouldn't even contemplate such an arrangement, and I so badly wanted to come.'

Adam felt frustrated. 'But where does my mother – or your father, for that matter – imagine you are?'

'I told them I was going to stay the week-end with a friend in Dublin. A taxi took me to the station and I took a train to Dublin. But I flew to London as well.'

'Don't you realize that was a completely irresponsible thing to do? A girl of your age travelling all that way – alone!'

Maria sighed. 'I'm not a child, Adam.'

'No, I can see that. Nevertheless, you're still not old enough to look after yourself properly.'

'Oh, Adam!' Maria pouted, her eyes flashing. 'Please, I've come to London for some freedom, not to be even more confined than I was in Kilcarney!'

Adam looked helplessly at Mrs. Lacey, and she said: 'Don't you think you ought to telephone your mother, doctor? She may be worried. If they should happen to have tried to contact Miss Maria . . .'

Adam gathered his thoughts, nodding decisively. 'Yes, you're right, Mrs. Lacey. I must do that. But as for you, young woman . . .' He shook his head. 'I don't know what to say.'

Maria tossed her head. 'Don't say anything, Adam, except that I can stay, and I shan't be any more trouble.'

Adam opened his mouth to protest and then closed it again. What was the use? She was here now, and after all, a little earlier he had been on the point of writing to tell his mother she could come. Certainly he had not imagined this situation being thrust upon him, or that Maria should look and act so differently from his expectations. Women were always unpredictable, he thought with male arrogance, and yet he had not expected Maria to appear womanly. He wasn't at all sure exactly what he had expected, maybe an enlargement of that picture he had of her in his mind's eye with a ponytail and a gymslip, but definitely not this confident creature, this product of her generation, with silky hair that tip-tilted slightly at the ends, and a taste in modern clothes that the inhabitants of Virginia Grove might find startling. Right now she was wearing a calf-length midi dress in a rather attractive shade of lovat, but its simple lines were not enhanced by the long front opening that revealed slender legs in knee-length soft leather boots. Adam shook his head a trifle resignedly. He could imagine with feeling Loren Griffiths' reactions to Maria Sheridan . . .

CHAPTER TWO

MARIA awoke with a start, and lay for a while wondering why there were no lace curtains at her windows, and why the coverlet on her bed was not the hand-woven one she had always been used to. Then realization of her surroundings came to her, and she moved pleasurably under the soft sheets, a smile curving her lips. Of course, she was no longer in Kilcarney, she was here in London, in Adam's house.

Her gaze drifted round the room, and she noted with pleasure the lemon striped curtains that matched the lemon bedspread, and the light teak veneer of the furniture. There was a soft, fluffy cream carpet on the floor, into which her toes had curled the night before, which seemed so much more luxurious than the woven carpets they had at home. But then her father was not one for appreciating such things. He was a very practical man in most things, preferring serviceability to artistic merit. Only the advent of Geraldine Massey into their lives had softened his attitudes slightly, and Maria had reason to be grateful to her stepmother for providing her with an ally. Over the years, it had been Geraldine who had interceded with her father on her behalf, and brought some measure of tolerance into their lives. And in this business of Maria coming to England, to take a secretarial course, Geraldine had been the prime mover.

Naturally, Maria had wanted to come. For years she had longed to escape from the confined life in Kilcarney where her father was a pillar of the community, and as such, unable to view any of his daughter's escapades with forbearance. But until now there had been no opportunity. She had been at the convent school, and surrounded by restrictions of one kind or another. But now she had left school and she was free to do as she wished, at least so long as her father was agreeable.

But it had been hard to convince him that no harm could come to her living with Adam, and she knew that if Adam should have shown any signs of misgivings regarding her proposed visit, her father would have overruled both Geraldine and herself and refused outright to allow her to come. That was why she had taken such a chance and deceived even her stepmother who might have felt it was her duty to inform her husband of what was going on.

Maria sighed and slid out of bed. Thankfully, she was here now, and if her father had sounded distrait on the telephone last evening at least he had not demanded that she should return immediately, and Maria knew that, given time, Geraldine would talk him round.

Now she padded to the window and looked out on to the small cul-de-sac below her windows. Unfastening the catch, she pushed up the window and leaned on the sill. The air was chill, and she shivered, but it was as much with anticipation as with the cold. Suddenly life was immensely exciting, and all sorts of possibilities were presenting themselves.

Suddenly she saw that an elderly woman across the Grove who had been on the point of gathering her milk bottles from her front step was regarding her disapprovingly and Maria glanced down at the scarcity of her attire hastily. She was merely dressed in the shortie nylon pyjamas she had worn to sleep in, and quickly she drew back and dropped the window, chuckling at her reflection in the mirror of the dressing table as she did so. It would never do to scandalize the neighbours on her first morning, and besides, no doubt they were all wondering who she was and why she was staying there. After all, Adam was a very eligible bachelor, and gossip was the breath of life to some people.

Shrugging, she went to wash in the huge bathroom that smelled pleasantly of shaving cream and after-shave lotion and then returned to fling open her suit-cases which she had left on the floor the night before. She rummaged through them for something to wear. Later she would unpack, but right now she was hungry. It was after eight o'clock, and at home she was used to breakfasting with her father about seven.

As she dressed she hoped she would have a chance to talk to Adam today. Last night he had been aloof and non-committal, asking the usual polite questions about their parents, but seemingly disinterested in herself. Of course, the call to Kilcarney had annoyed him, but that was only to be expected. Then he had disappeared to take evening surgery at his clinic which Mrs. Lacey had told her was in the East End of London, Maria couldn't remember the name, and later when she had expected him back the housekeeper had informed her that he was dining out. Altogether it had been a most unsatisfactory evening, and she determined to change that today.

Now, dressed in close-fitting denim pants in a rather vivid shade of purple and a cream shirt that reached her hips and was belted at the waist, her straight hair swinging to her shoulders, she descended the staircase to the hall below. She wore no make-up, but her skin

24

was naturally smooth anyway.

She hesitated in the hall, looking about her with interest. The carpet here, as on the stairs, was patterned in blues and greens, while all the doors were panelled in a light wood. There was a polished chest on which reposed a vase of tulips and narcissi, and their pale colours looked well against the darker wood.

As she stood there, speculating as to whether Adam breakfasted in the same room as she had dined the night before, Mrs. Lacey emerged from the kitchen to regard her with some trepidation.

'Oh – you're up, miss,' she said unnecessarily. 'I – er – I was about to bring you up a tray. The doctor said you might be tired after your journey.'

Maria smiled charmingly. 'I'm not tired, Mrs. Lacey,' she averred firmly, shaking her head. 'I feel marvellous!' She stretched her arms unselfconsciously above her head. 'Tell me, Mrs. Lacey, where is Adam?'

Mrs. Lacey tried to hide her disapproval. She was obviously very much aware of the purple trousers, and Maria, sensing this, hid a smile. 'Mr. Adam is just finishing his breakfast, miss. In . . . in here.'

She moved forward to thrust open the door of the dining-room where Maria had eaten her solitary meal the evening before, and Maria nodded her thanks and entered the room quietly.

Adam was engrossed in his morning newspaper, and with his back to the door barely noticed anyone's entrance. Obviously, he might expect Mrs. Lacey to return to ascertain he had everything he needed, but no one else. Dressed in a dark suit, his linen immaculately white against the darker skin of his neck, Maria thought he looked very cool, and very dark and very

25

businesslike, and a feeling of excitement rippled through her. With her usual lack of inhibition, she walked across the carpeted floor to him and bending, slid her arms round his neck from behind, kissing him warmly against the side of his neck as she sometimes did her father.

Adam jerked out of her grasp in a jack-knife movement to get to his feet and stare at her angrily. '*Maria!*' he snapped shortly, thrusting his paper to one side and raking one hand through his thick hair.

She smiled enchantingly. 'Good morning, Adam,' she said, taking the vacant seat to one side of the chair he had been occupying. 'I'm sorry I'm late for breakfast.'

Adam seemed to gather his composure, and breathing heavily, considered her impatiently. 'You're not late,' he replied bleakly. 'There's absolutely no need for you to rise this early. But I have to be away to the surgery by eight-thirty.'

Maria shrugged and reaching for the coffee pot poured herself a cup of coffee with the ease of one used to the practice, and Adam felt the rising sense of frustration he had felt at her attitude the previous evening. 'But I want to get up this early,' she said, sipping her coffee. 'Besides, it will be nice for you having company for a change. Your mother said she always breakfasted with you.'

'That's a little different,' returned Adam dryly, lifting his coffee cup and finishing its contents with a gulp.

Maria raised her eyebrows. 'I don't see why it should be. I am your sister, after all.'

'My stepsister!' Adam corrected her harshly.

'That's splitting hairs!' she observed lightly. 'That's

your mother's expression, by the way.' She chuckled. 'Hm, this coffee is quite good, but – ugh – do you eat a fried breakfast?'

Adam controlled his annoyance. 'That's my business.'

Maria shrugged. 'I suppose it is. Do you think Mrs. Lacey will expect me to do the same?'

'Perhaps you should ask her that.' Adam was abrupt.

Maria sighed and regarded him resignedly. 'Aren't you going to sit down again, Adam?'

Adam made a point of looking at his wrist watch. 'I don't have time,' he replied, without any trace of apology in his voice.

Maria sighed again, more pronouncedly, and said: 'Oh, well, I'll just have some coffee, and I'll be with you.'

Adam had turned away to examine some papers in his briefcase, but he turned at her words to regard her uncomprehendingly. 'What do you mean?'

Maria poured more coffee into her cup. 'I want to come with you this morning – to your surgery, I mean. I want to see where you work, and I might even be able to help you.'

Adam was astounded. 'Thank you, but that won't be necessary, Maria. I have a very adequate receptionist to deal with my affairs. You must entertain yourself as best you can.'

Maria's cup clattered into its saucer. 'But I want to come with you, Adam.'

'Well, you can't.' Adam shook his head. 'And I should change those clothes before you go anywhere, if I were you.'

'What's wrong with my clothes?' Maria got to her

feet slowly.

'If you don't know then I don't have the time to tell you,' retorted Adam, rather cruelly.

Maria clenched her fists. 'You're just like my father!' she exclaimed angrily. She compressed her lips for a moment, and then an unwilling smile lifted their corners. 'I know you're only trying to annoy me!' she said. 'Maybe you expect me to say I won't come with you, is that it?'

Adam gave her an exasperated look, and then turned and walked out into the hall, almost bumping into Mrs. Lacey as she came to see what Maria wanted to eat. But to her surprise, Maria herself followed Adam into the hall, and lifted the orange anorak from its place in the hall closet.

Adam, who had pulled on a sheepskin car coat over his suit, turned to regard her impatiently. 'You can't come, Maria,' he said firmly, his voice cold. 'I'm sorry, but my surgery is no place for a – a – girl like you.' He had been about to say child, but thought better of it.

Maria's eyes mirrored their hurt, and he studied her for a long moment before saying: 'I'm sorry,' again, and turning, he walked to the front door. The door slammed behind him and Maria wrinkled her nose to hide the disappointment she was feeling. Then she tugged off her anorak and threw it back into the closet, not bothering to pick it up when it fell on to the floor, and Mrs. Lacey hurried forward and lifted it herself, feeling an unwilling sense of compassion for the girl.

Maria walked moodily back into the dining-room, her hands thrust deep into the hip pockets of her trousers, and wondered with a bleak sense of isolation whether she had done the right thing by coming here.

Then she pushed the thought aside and lifted Adam's newspaper. Turning it to the first page, she flung herself into his chair and made a brave attempt to read it. Mrs. Lacey, coming in a few moments later and encountering her brooding gaze, wondered whether she had been mistaken in thinking she had seen pain in Maria's amber eyes.

'What would you like to eat, miss?' she asked, beginning to clear Adam's dirty plates on to her tray.

Maria looked up reluctantly. She didn't feel like talking to anybody right now. 'Nothing, thank you,' she replied politely, and Mrs. Lacey looked at her doubtfully.

'Don't you think you ought to have something, miss?' she asked. 'A young girl like you. You must he hungry.'

Maria compressed her lips again. 'I was,' she admitted quietly. 'But not now.'

Mrs. Lacey sighed, putting down the tray and folding her arms. 'Now that's silly, miss, if you don't mind me saying so. Saying you don't want food just because Mr. Adam wouldn't take you with him—'

Maria's eyes widened. 'I didn't mention Adam,' she said, with an attempt at coolness.

Mrs. Lacey shook her head. 'No, of course you didn't. But that's what's wrong, I can tell. You wanted to help, that's all, but you can't, so you might as well make the best of a bad job.'

Maria looked at her distantly, and then her mobile face broke into a grudging smile. It was not in her nature to remain moody for long, and it wasn't Mrs. Lacey's fault after all. 'All right,' she agreed, with a sigh. 'I did want to go. But I couldn't, and now I don't feel very hungry.'

'Well, what about some cereal? Or perhaps a little bacon.'

Maria looked horrified at this. 'Oh, no,' she cried. 'But maybe some toast.'

Mrs. Lacey nodded. 'All right, miss. Some toast, and perhaps a little of my home-made marmalade.'

Maria smiled. 'That sounds delicious!'

After breakfast, Maria asked the housekeeper whether there was anything she could do around the house. Mrs. Lacey looked surprised, and said: 'Like what, miss?'

Maria frowned. 'I could make the beds,' she volunteered, 'or perhaps you would like me to do the washing up. I can cook, too.'

Mrs. Lacey was obviously taken aback. Guests did not usually offer their services around the house, but the idea was not unpleasant. Even so . . . 'That's very kind of you, miss,' she replied, rather flustered, 'but it's not necessary, you know. This isn't a large house and caring for one man doesn't take a lot of doing.'

'But there's two of us now,' pointed out Maria, but Mrs. Lacey still shook her head.

'It's very kind of you, miss, but I don't think Mr. Adam would approve. In any case, you haven't been out of doors since you arrived yesterday afternoon. How would you like to go down to the shops in the High Street, and fetch me some things I need?'

'Shopping?' Maria hesitated. 'Oh, yes, I should like that.'

'Good.' Mrs. Lacey was relieved to have found a solution to Maria's problem, and in the kitchen she made out a list of her requirements. Later, armed with a shopping basket and Mrs. Lacey's purse, Maria made her way, following the housekeeper's directions, to the

High Street.

It was a beautiful spring morning now that the early chill had dissipated, and Maria's sense of well-being returned. It was natural that Adam should find it difficult to adapt to having someone else living in his house, particularly as that someone was also related to him, if only by marriage. She must not expect to make too many demands on him all at once. A doctor's life was not like that of a farmer. He had no set hours, and the responsibilities he carried were bound to make him more serious.

In this happy mood she did her tour of the shops, using her innate country sense of shrewdness when it came to deciding which cuts of meat to buy and which vegetables to choose. She insisted on handling the tomatoes before buying them, much to the dealer's annoyance, but at least she had the satisfaction at the end of knowing she had not been cheated. In her orange anorak and the purple pants she did not look out of place in the High Street where all manner of attire could be seen, but as she turned again into Virginia Grove she observed several slightly raised eyebrows among the tenants who were out and about. Mrs. Lacey was amazed at how little Maria had spent on her purchases, half expecting the girl to come back without half the things she had been sent for. Now she made them some coffee and as they sat companionably at the breakfast bar in the kitchen, chatting, Mrs. Lacey found out a little about Maria's background and of her life in Kilcarney.

After a while Maria skilfully changed the subject and said: 'What time does Adam come home for lunch?'

Mrs. Lacey smiled and slipped off her stool, carrying

her empty cup to the sink unit. 'Oh, about one o'clock,' she replied. 'But he doesn't always come home for lunch.'

'Oh!' Maria could scarcely hide her disappointment, and Mrs. Lacey went on to say that when he wasn't coming home he usually telephoned before eleven. 'And has he phoned today?' Maria couldn't help asking.

Mrs. Lacey shook her head. 'No, miss. He'll be home. After all, afternoons are his only free time until the evening. He has quite a practice, he and Mr. Hadley and Mr. Vincent.'

'Who are they?'

'His partners.'

'Oh, I see,' Maria nodded. 'And the practice is in Islington, is that right?'

'Yes, miss.'

'Where is that?'

'It's over towards the East End, beyond Camden Town, miss. Not a particularly nice area, but a big population.'

Maria frowned. 'The East End? My stepmother said there were a lot of slums there.'

'So there are, and a lot of them are in Islington.'

'But why don't they do something about it?'

'They are. Eventually all those old tenement buildings will be pulled down and there'll be flats and things, miss. It's just that it's easier said than done.'

'And Adam works there.' Maria stared at Mrs. Lacey. 'Why?'

Mrs. Lacey folded her arms. 'He knows that's where he's most needed, miss. Terrible place for illness, damp houses are. There are a lot of old people there, too. Live alone, a lot of them. Like this Mrs. Ainsley, who's in St.

Michael's right now.'

'Mrs. Ainsley?'

'Yes, she's an old lady of about seventy. Lives alone, she does. Got this old dog, Minstrel. Anyway, last week she tripped at the top of the stairs and fell right down.'

'Oh, that's terrible,' said Maria, pressing a hand to her throat. 'Is – is she very badly injured?'

'Well, she's alive. But there were internal injuries, you know. Bleeding, she was, when they found her.'

Maria shook her head. 'And who found her?'

'The doctor himself. He was used to calling on her, just for a visit. He used to say she needed someone. But anyway, she's in the hospital now, and God knows when she'll get out, poor soul.'

Maria bit her lip. 'Has she no family?'

Mrs. Lacey considered. 'I don't think so. Not in this country anyway. She did have a daughter, but she emigrated some time ago.'

Maria sighed, cupping her chin on one hand. 'I think I should like to work with people,' she said. 'It must be very rewarding, helping someone like that.'

Mrs. Lacey raised her eyebrows in surprise. 'But I thought you'd come here to England to take a secretarial course at the commercial college?'

Maria smiled. 'I have. At least, that's what Geraldine thought I would enjoy doing. But after listening to you, I'm not so sure. There must be hundreds of old people, like this Mrs. Ainsley. Perhaps there are opportunities in that kind of social work—'

Mrs. Lacey looked anxious. 'Now don't you go getting all romantic about caring for people and sorting out their troubles,' she said. 'It's not all that easy. You have to have the patience of Job.'

Maria raised her eyebrows. 'I suppose you're right. Back home families are larger and usually someone is only too willing to care for the old folk. My grandmother is still alive, and lives in a cottage not far from my father. He wouldn't dream of cutting her off by moving away.'

Mrs. Lacey sighed. 'No, well, things are different here. People don't have time to do everything they should do. They're too busy trying to better their neighbours. They don't realize that they'll be old, too, one day.'

Maria traced the pattern of the formica on the breakfast bar with an idle forefinger. 'Still, I suppose so far as I'm concerned you're right. But I can't help feeling sorry for people.'

Mrs. Lacey's expression softened. 'Don't be too vulnerable,' she advised quietly. 'There's always someone ready and willing to take advantage of you.'

Maria smiled, 'That sounds very cynical.'

'Perhaps I am, at that.' Mrs. Lacey shrugged. 'Working here as Mr. Adam's housekeeper, I see quite a lot of hardship, but not everybody deserves the help they're given. You go and take your office course, like you planned. That way you'll keep out of mischief.'

Maria looked indignant. 'I can take care of myself.'

Mrs. Lacey looked sceptical. 'Can you? I'm not so sure. Not here, anyway. London's not all Changing the Guard and Buckingham Palace, you know.'

'And I'm not still wet behind the ears,' replied Maria shortly.

'Nobody said you were. But just by having you here, Mr. Adam's letting himself in for a lot of extra responsibility, and he works hard enough as it is.'

34

Maria sighed and slid off her stool. She had had enough of this conversation. She remembered her suitcases, still not unpacked, upstairs. She could go and deal with them before lunch, and possibly find something different to wear. Something Adam might not find so objectionable.

But even as she was about to mention her plans to Mrs. Lacey the front door bell rang, and Mrs. Lacey sighed in annoyance. 'Oh, will you go and answer that?' she asked of Maria. 'My hands are wet. If it's someone for the doctor you'll have to ask them to come back later.'

'All right.' Maria nodded and walked out into the hall. Smoothing her hair, she opened the door and stared in some surprise at the woman who was tapping her foot impatiently as she waited outside. Somehow she had not expected to find anyone so decorative on Adam's doorstep, and this woman was most certainly that. Small, and delicately proportioned, with silky golden hair bound into a coronet on top of her head, she was quite beautiful, but her expression as she stared appraisingly at Maria was not pleasant.

'Yes?' Maria looked at her expectantly. 'Can I help you?'

The woman glanced back down Adam's drive, and now Maria noticed a chauffeur-driven limousine at the gates. The woman looked again at her and said: 'You must be Maria. Adam's told me about you.'

Maria managed a faint smile. 'Oh, yes. Er – won't you come in?' She felt obliged to invite the woman in, for she was obviously no ordinary patient of Adam's.

The woman's lips parted in a semblance of a smile and she stepped into the hall. Her entry brought Mrs. Lacey to the kitchen door and when she saw who the visitor was she wiped her hands on her apron and came through.

'Oh, it's you, Miss Griffiths,' she said politely. 'I'm afraid you're too early for Mr. Adam.'

Loren drew off her pearl grey gloves. 'But I didn't come primarily to see Adam,' she replied smoothly. 'I wanted to – meet – Maria.'

'I see.' Mrs. Lacey glanced doubtfully at the girl. 'And does Mr. Adam know you're here, miss?'

Loren raised her dark eyebrows. 'I hardly think so. Does it matter?' Her voice was cool. 'I'm sure he won't object, Mrs. Lacey.' She regarded the older woman challengingly and Mrs. Lacey's gaze fell before Loren's persistent stare.

'No, miss,' Mrs. Lacey agreed at last. 'Er – would you like some coffee?'

Loren shrugged. 'If it's not too much trouble, Mrs. Lacey.'

Mrs. Lacey sniffed and without another word marched back into the kitchen. 'Ignorant old woman!' remarked Loren maliciously, and Maria felt her own cheeks burning as she overheard the comment. Then Loren turned to her and said: 'As Mrs. Lacey has omitted to introduce us, I suppose I had better do it myself. I'm Loren Griffiths!'

She said the name as though she expected it to have some effect on Maria, but Maria merely managed a faint smile and Loren went on: 'Has Adam mentioned me?'

Maria twisted her hands together. 'I'm afraid not. But then it's several years since I last saw him, and I only arrived yesterday afternoon.'

'Ah, yes.' Loren smiled rather sardonically. 'Well, shall we go into the lounge?'

Maria moved forward quickly, apologetically. 'Oh, yes, of course,' she said hastily, not altogether sure how to treat this woman who seemed to know her step-brother so intimately, and was quite at home in his house.

Loren preceded her into the low, light lounge that faced the gardens at the back of the house. It was a pleasant room furnished simply and comfortably with black buttoned leather couches and a cream and gold patterned carpet on the floor. Here Adam had a television and a radiogram, and there were bookshelves filled with every kind of literature, as Maria had discovered the night before. French doors opened on to a small patio, where there were tubs of climbing plants and a trellis overgrown with rambling roses.

Loren seated herself comfortably on the couch, opening her coat to reveal a short-skirted woollen dress in an attractive shade of turquoise, and indicated that Maria should take the chair opposite. But in this Maria thwarted her, pretending not to see her gesture. She was somehow loath to sit down to what might well turn out to be a kind of refined catechism. Obviously this woman had come here out of curiosity to see what Adam's stepsister was really like, and although Maria could understand her curiosity, she couldn't help feeling this visit was precipitate. However, she did come to stand by the screened fireplace, smiling cautiously at her guest and wondering exactly what her relationship was to Adam.

Loren herself seemed completely at ease, lighting a cigarette which she had extracted from the heavy box on the low table in front of her and drawing on it to her satisfaction. Maria waited patiently for her to speak, and presently Loren said:

'I suppose Adam was quite surprised to find you here yesterday, wasn't he?'

Maria smiled and relaxed a little. 'Oh, *yes*,' she agreed, with candour. 'I don't think he was particularly pleased about it.'

Loren studied her intently. 'Perhaps not. Didn't it occur to you to consider that it would have been more diplomatic to wait until you were actually invited?'

Maria was taken aback. 'No. I didn't think it was necessary,' she replied. 'Adam is my brother.'

'He is your stepbrother, which is quite a different thing.'

'Nevertheless, he is a part of my family.'

'A part you don't know very well, I would hazard a guess,' observed Loren a little dryly.

'Perhaps so. I intend to remedy that,' replied Maria, aroused by the other woman's scornful manner.

Loren inhaled deeply and at that moment Mrs. Lacey came in with the tray of coffee. She placed it on the table beside Loren and straightened stiffly. 'Is there anything else you require, miss?'

Loren glanced at the tray. 'No, thank you, Mrs. Lacey. That looks perfect.'

Mrs. Lacey nodded briefly and withdrew, and Maria looked after her rather doubtfully. She wondered whether Mrs. Lacey approved of her entertaining this woman in Adam's house and in his absence. Had she been mistaken in thinking that Loren Griffiths was a friend of Adam's?

Loren poured out the coffee, but Maria refused to have any. She had already had some with Mrs. Lacey, and besides, she had no particular desire to be sociable with this woman. There was something about her manner that she didn't like, although apart from a few observations Loren had said nothing offensive. Yet she had the feeling she was being thoroughly appraised and she wondered again why she should have wanted to meet her. They seemed to have nothing in common.

'What course are you planning to take?' Loren interrupted her train of thought with a question.

Maria shrugged. 'I'm not sure yet, Miss Griffiths. I've made no definite plans.'

'I see.' Loren frowned. 'I should have thought it would have been more convenient for you to take such a course nearer your own home. After all, they do have that sort of thing there, don't they?' She said it as though Ireland was inhabited by primitives.

Maria nodded politely, however, and said: 'Yes, there are courses there, but I wanted to come to London.'

'I see,' Loren said again. 'Even so, you must admit, coming here to live with your stepbrother is rather – how shall I put it? – unconventional.'

Maria felt her cheeks colouring. 'Is it, Miss Griffiths?'

'Don't you think so?'

'*No!*'

Loren sighed, pressing out her cigarette impatiently. 'You're obviously not a child, Maria. Surely you can see that it would have been far more suitable for you to share a flat with several other girls than living here with Adam?'

Maria stiffened. Such an idea had never entered her head, and besides, she knew her father would never have countenanced such a suggestion. In consequence, her young voice was heated as she retorted: 'I don't see what business it is of yours, Miss Griffiths, where I choose to make my home!'

'Maria!' The unexpectedly male voice startled both of them, and Maria swung round to find Adam standing in the doorway to the lounge, his face dark and annoyed. They must have been so absorbed in their argument that they had not heard him enter the house.

Loren immediately got to her feet and before Maria could speak she rushed across to him eagerly. 'Adam! Darling!' she exclaimed, her voice soft and appealing, much different from the rather harsh tones she had used to Maria. 'I've been waiting for you.'

Adam regarded her sardonically for a moment, restraining with his arm any attempt she might have made to embrace him. Then he looked across at Maria questioningly. Maria twisted her hands behind her back and lifted her shoulders in a defiant shrug. She had no intention of trying to make explanations while Loren Griffiths was there.

As though sensing her withdrawal, Adam looked back at the woman who was clinging to his arm, and his eyes softened. 'Well, Loren?' he said challengingly. 'Exactly why are you here? Or can I guess?'

Loren made an eloquent gesture, and realizing he was not in a mood to be cajoled, decided to be honest. 'I came to meet Maria,' she said coolly. 'After all, I am your fiancée, aren't I, darling?'

'Are you?' Adam was equally as cool, annoyingly so.

Loren sighed. 'Of course I am.' She looked across at Maria. 'Perhaps you ought to explain that to your – er – stepsister!'

Maria controlled herself with difficulty. Loren was being openly insolent now, secure in the knowledge of Adam's support. Even so, Adam didn't appear at all amused by the situation, and she could only assume he was still angry with her for speaking to his fiancée as she had done. He should have told her he was engaged. He should have explained that his fiancée might call. He should not have allowed her to be placed in such an embarrassing position.

With a muffled, 'Excuse me,' she walked quickly across the room, brushing past them to escape into the hall. Once there, she made a hasty retreat to her bedroom, slamming the door rather harder than was necessary. Then she glared at her reflection in the dressing table mirror. All of a sudden she didn't like today either . . .

CHAPTER THREE

IT was with some reluctance that Maria eventually came down for lunch. In her room she had unpacked her cases and hung her clothes away in the wardrobe, but she had little heart in the task. If Loren Griffiths had her way she would use her influence with Adam to have Maria sent back to Kilcarney, and the realization of this infuriated her.

Thrusting these thoughts aside, she had washed and changed into a short-skirted tangerine dress that drew attention to the slender length of her legs, and brushed her hair until it shone. Even so, it was not until Mrs. Lacey called: 'Miss Maria! Lunch is ready!' that she ventured downstairs.

As she entered the dining-room, she assumed a defiant expression, but she needn't have bothered because she was alone. However, the table was set for two and a puzzled frown marred her smooth forehead. Hearing steps behind her, she swung round expecting to see Mrs. Lacey, but it was Adam himself who came into the room, and she felt the hot colour run annoyingly up her cheeks.

'Sit down!' he said, indicating the chairs at the table, and Maria decided to obey rather than create any kind of argument then. Adam went to help himself to a whisky at the drinks cabinet to one side of the windows, and Maria watched him with some impatience. Would he ask her to join him? And where was Loren Griffiths?

Adam returned to the table, swallowing half his

whisky and placing his glass on the table. Seating himself, he regarded Maria sombrely, and she fidgeted with her napkin, wishing he would say something – *anything*.

Finally she asked: 'Where is Miss Griffiths?'

Adam lifted his shoulders in a casual gesture. 'Keeping an appointment with her producer, I believe,' he replied.

'Her producer?' Maria licked her upper lip thoughtfully. 'What is she? Some kind of actress?'

Adam's expression grew slightly mocking. 'You mean you haven't heard of her?'

'Should I have done?'

He frowned consideringly. 'Perhaps not. Her reputation has been made mostly here and in the United States. She's had considerable success there.'

'I see.' Maria nodded. 'I thought she expected some kind of recognition from me. I think I disappointed her, Adam.'

His eyes narrowed. 'Well, I suppose that's one way of putting it,' he remarked mildly. 'Tell me, exactly what was going on when I arrived to interrupt you?'

Maria's cheeks turned a brilliant red. 'Didn't she tell you?'

'If she had, would I be asking?'

'I don't know. You might. You might expect me to lie about it.'

'Now why would you do that?'

Maria lifted her shoulders defensively. 'Oh, well, she said I shouldn't have come here uninvited, and that I ought to have found a flat to share with some girls of my own age.'

'Did she now?' Adam sounded intensely interested. 'And what was your reaction to that?'

43

Maria compressed her lips. 'You heard it,' she said shortly.

'Ah!' Adam nodded. 'Well, I'm glad you've explained, at any rate. I prefer the truth to prevarication. Remember that, will you?'

Mrs. Lacey came in with their meal at that moment, and for a time there was silence as they tackled the delicious lunch the housekeeper had prepared. Then Maria said:

'You didn't tell your mother you were engaged to be married, did you?'

Adam looked up. 'No,' he agreed.

'Why?' Maria bit her lip. 'If you had explained I shouldn't have said what I did.'

Adam lay back lazily in his chair. 'You must know my mother very well by this time. Would you say she would approve of Loren?'

Maria rested her elbows on the table and cupped her chin on her hands. 'I don't know. Perhaps. Surely the most important thing is whether you would be happy with her.'

Adam raised his eyebrows. 'Such worldly wisdom!' he observed.

Maria sighed. 'I don't think she would make you happy,' she volunteered truthfully.

Adam stared at her exasperatedly. 'I don't recall asking for your opinion.'

'No, but I've given it, for what it's worth.' Maria studied her fingernails. 'Have – have you known Miss Griffiths long?'

'A year,' replied Adam briefly, and Maria knew she had annoyed him again.

He rose from his seat a few moments later before Mrs. Lacey returned with their coffee, and Maria watched him with some exasperation. Surely he was not about to desert her again? Getting up, she came round the table, linking her fingers together nervously.

'I'm sorry,' she began, sighing. 'I've annoyed you, haven't I?'

Adam looked at her impatiently. 'You provoke me, Maria,' he replied shortly. 'I'm not at all convinced Loren isn't right in her suggestion that you might be better off sharing a flat with girls of your own age.'

Maria's brows drew together. 'You can't be serious!'

Adam regarded her intently, and shrugged his broad shoulders. 'Why not? You must admit your arrival here was a trifle precipitate!'

Maria compressed her lips impotently, anger rising inside her at his hurtful words. 'You're deliberately trying to provoke me, now,' she accused him hotly.

Adam raked a hand through his thick hair. Maybe she was right. Maybe he was being deliberately cruel, but if he was, it was because her directness aroused his irritation.

With an exclamation he turned away, hearing the telephone begin to ring with some relief. He opened the door and went to answer it, and when he came back Mrs. Lacey was with him, carrying the tray of coffee.

'Oh, surely you don't have to rush out without even having your coffee, doctor,' she was protesting, and Adam was apologizing but explaining that the call was urgent.

Maria stood unhappily watching them. 'What is it? What's wrong?' she asked, and Adam shifted his gaze to her for a moment.

'One of my patients has had a heart attack,' he replied briefly. 'I'm sorry to have to dash off like this, but I'm afraid it's all part of the romance of a doctor's life!' His tone was sardonic and Maria was quite sure he was glad of the chance to escape any further conversation with her.

She scarcely made any response, and a few minutes later she heard the roar of the Rover's engine as he backed it expertly out of the drive.

During the afternoon, Maria decided to go out.

Mrs. Lacey wasn't at all happy about her venturing far alone, but Maria disregarded her anxious admonitions and taking only a long knitted jacket for her shoulders went out about two o'clock. She felt sick and fed up, and very much out of sorts with herself. It was impossible to consider that this time yesterday she had been full of excitement and anticipation when now she felt so morose and dejected.

She tried to remember more about the times Adam had visited Kilcarney, but it was difficult finding any comparisons between the man she had known then and the man she knew now. Her impressions then had been those of a schoolgirl, and naturally she had found his greater age and experience rather awe-inspiring. Even so, he had been human and kind, and over the years she had built up a picture of him as a friendly, attractive person, willing to listen to her and interested in her aspirations. How different he was, persisting to regard her as a rather trying nuisance the responsibility for whom had been thrust upon him unwillingly. For the first time, she wondered whether he would have refused to allow her to come had she waited for his reply to her stepmother's letter. Had she been precipitate, as he had said? She sighed. Either way, it didn't matter now, and all of a sudden she felt immensely homesick for the warmth and familiarity of her father's house.

She paused in the High Street, uncertain of her surroundings, and wished she had thought to buy a guide book. But somehow she had always imagined that Adam would be there to show her around, and never had she thought he might regard her as nothing but a liability.

She began to walk rather aimlessly, following the main street without much enthusiasm, but eventually it brought her to Piccadilly and in spite of herself she became interested in exploring the tourist meccas. There was something pleasantly soothing about being in a crowd, losing one's identity in the masses. After all, this was the city she had read about so avidly; 'swinging' London, as the guide books all boasted. It didn't 'swing' much as far as Maria could see, and yet she sensed the warmth of its people and some of her homesickness fled away.

She spent the afternoon wandering from place to place, gazing with wonder at the ancient buildings that were all that was left of the turbulent past. She stood for a while on Tower Bridge watching the barges passing beneath its shadow and staring at the tall blackened walls of the Tower itself. History had always been one of her favourite subjects and she knew well the terrible crimes that had been committed in those dungeons. Another day she would go into the Tower and see the Crown Jewels and maybe stand in the yard where two of England's Queens were beheaded. English history was so fascinating and it was easy to feel the spell of timelessness in places like this. There were lots of places she wanted to see, and although she had enjoyed herself this afternoon it would have been so much more exciting if there had been someone with her with whom to share it all. As it was, as the sun began to slide down the sky, her depression returned as she faced the prospect of another lonely dinner while Adam went about his own affairs.

Tears pricked her eyes, but she pushed them back and started to walk again. She must not cry. She must not give in to self-pity like this. It was her own fault that she was here, and she must just make the best of it if she intended to stay. If . . .

In Piccadilly Circus she stood feeling totally bewildered as hordes of commuters streamed past her on their way to bus and tube stations. She knew she ought to call a taxi and get home that way, for she was no longer certain of her whereabouts, but the chances of her being able to attract a cab-driver's attention at this peak hour were slight. So she made her way to a small cafeteria and ordered coffee and doughnuts and decided to wait.

It was quite pleasant, sitting in the window seat watching the crowds making their way home. She didn't feel so aimless there and no one was pushing or jostling her. She drank her coffee slowly and gradually it was possible to see a slowing of the traffic. By the time she had finished her third cup of coffee, it was possible to walk outside without difficulty, and she thrust her hands into the pockets of her long woollen jacket and walked in the direction of Hyde Park.

Her legs were aching by this time, and she sat down on a bench and took off one shoe and examined her blistered heel. Until then she had not realized how painful her feet actually were, and she decided she would have to take a taxi home after all.

An elderly woman came and sat down beside her, smiling at her rather sympathetically. 'Well now, they look pretty uncomfortable, my dear,' she said, nodding at Maria's blisters.

Maria managed a smile. 'They are,' she admitted, wincing as she slid her foot back into her shoe. 'I've been walking about all afternoon.'

The woman studied her appraisingly. 'Have you, dear? Not English, are you?'

Maria shook her head. 'No, I'm from Ireland.'

The woman nodded comfortably. 'I thought so. New to London, I suppose, dear?'

'Oh, yes.' Maria sighed. 'It's such a big place, isn't it?'

'It is that. And hard when you don't know anyone. What are you here for? Looking for a job? Waiting on, most likely. In hotels?'

Maria shook her head. 'Oh, no. I want to take a secretarial course.' She frowned. 'I'd like to work in an office.'

The woman watched her intently. 'Is that so? Working in an office, eh? You don't hanker after the bright lights, then?'

Maria smiled. 'I don't think so.'

The woman stared at her penetratingly. 'And what if I was to tell you that I might be able to find you a job, office work of course, without there being any need for the kind of formal training you're on about?'

Maria's eyes widened. 'A job? In an office? Could you?'

'As it happens, I might. I've a friend, see, needs a pretty girl like you to do his filing and so on. Easy work, good pay, better prospects! Just the thing for a girl like

49

yourself.'

Maria was taken aback. 'I don't know what to say.'

The woman smiled and patted her hand. 'Don't say anything, dear. Just give me your name and I'll give my friend a ring and make arrangements for you—'

A shadow fell across them as they sat there and Maria looked up in surprise. A tall policeman was standing in front of them looking down at them solemnly.

'Now then, Beatrice,' he said heavily, 'what's going on here? Up to your old tricks, are you?'

The woman got to her feet, brushing down her coat defensively. 'I don't know what you mean, officer,' she said haughtily. 'I was just sitting here, minding my own business, passing the time of day with this young lady.'

'Is that right, miss?' The policeman looked at Maria. 'She wasn't offering you a job, was she?'

Maria's eyes were eloquent, and the policeman looked resignedly at the woman he had called Beatrice. 'Oh, dear me, Beatrice,' he said. 'And after all you promised . . .'

The woman give Maria an angry stare. 'I haven't done nothing. Did she say I'd offered her a job?'

'She didn't have to,' retorted the policeman, shaking his head.

'Well, are you making a charge?'

The policeman frowned. 'That rather depends.'

'Depends on what?'

'Depends on what kind of a job you were offering her.'

Maria listened to this interchange with a rising sense of anxiety. What was going on? What was this all about? Why was the policeman asking all these questions? What had the woman done?

Now he turned to Maria. 'Well, miss,' he said, 'what did she say?'

Maria's disturbed gaze moved from the policeman's expectant face to that of the woman's. All trace of friendliness had disappeared and she was looking at Maria with something like fear in her eyes. All of a sudden, Maria didn't want to be involved.

'I don't know,' she said now, to the policeman. 'I really don't know.'

The policeman straightened and regarded Beatrice with resignation. 'You're lucky,' he said harshly. 'Bloody lucky!'

Beatrice compressed her lips. 'I was doing no harm,' she insisted. 'Can I go now?'

The policeman shrugged and looked again at Maria. 'I suppose so,' he said. 'Yes – get along with you.'

The woman walked away quickly, wrapping her coat closer about her, and the policeman looked down at Maria with troubled eyes. 'Now then,' he said, 'where have you come from?'

Maria swallowed hard. 'Ken – Kensington,' she stammered.

'What are you doing up west?'

'I – I've been sightseeing,' she replied.

'On your own?'

'Yes.'

'Don't you have no mum or dad?'

'Not in England, no.'

The policeman shook his head heavily. 'You living alone, then?'

'No, I live with my stepbrother.'

'In Kensington?'

'Yes. He's a doctor.'

'And he lets you come up here, running into all sorts of trouble?' The policeman looked astounded.

Maria swallowed again. 'I don't understand. I was just sitting here, resting my feet, when that woman came and spoke to me. I thought she was just being kind and friendly.'

The policeman gave her a pitying glance. 'Oh, yes, Beatrice would be very kind and friendly,' he agreed dryly. 'At least till she'd persuaded you you were wasting your time trying to make a decent living in this place!'

Maria got rather unsteadily to her feet. 'Excuse me?' she said shakily. 'I don't understand.'

The policeman sighed. 'Surely you know what I'm talking about? A kid of your age? You know the facts of life, don't you?'

'What?' Maria stared at him incredulously. Then she pressed a hand to her mouth, feeling slightly sick. 'You don't mean—'

'Oh, but I do.' The policeman stared at her exasperatedly. 'Look, you go and get a bus or a tube home, eh? Cut along back to that stepbrother of yours. I'd like to give him a piece of my mind. And remember, don't – repeat don't – speak to strangers in the park again.'

Maria felt a great wave of horror sweep over her, and with a jerky nodding of her head she left him, scurrying away towards the road. All of a sudden she was frightened and Adam's house beckoned like a blessed sanctuary in all this alien city.

The taxis were empty now, and she hailed one easily, huddling into the corner after she had given the driver her address. She thought he looked at her rather doubtfully, but he made no comment and when they reached the Grove she climbed out on trembling legs. She managed to find enough change to pay him, and then stumbled up the drive to the house. As she fumbled with the handle of the door, it was suddenly wrenched open, and she almost fell into Adam's arms.

'For the love of God, where have you been—' he began fiercely, and then saw her pale, terrified face and dragged her inside unceremoniously, slamming the door behind them.

Maria stood shivering apprehensively, and he muttered an exclamation and strode ahead of her into the lounge. 'Come in here!' he commanded, when she did not immediately follow him, and with slow reluctant steps she obeyed.

He was pouring out a measure of brandy into a glass and as she hovered uncertainly just inside the door he thrust the glass into her hand and said: 'Drink that! You look ghastly.'

Maria did as she was told, although the harsh spirit caused her to cough for a moment as it burned its way down into her stomach. Adam stood watching her broodingly, and as the warmth of the brandy burned its way through her system she realized what a sorry picture she must appear. Finishing the drink, she handed him back the glass, and he held it between his fingers, continuing to look at her expectantly.

'Well?' he said, in a controlled voice. 'Are you feeling ready to make some explanations now?'

Maria moved defensively. 'Have – have you been worried about me?'

Adam bit off an expletive. 'Do you realize it's almost eight o'clock?' he snapped savagely. 'I've been half out of my mind with worry about you, and you dare to stand there and ask that!'

Maria quivered under his piercing gaze. 'I – I'm sorry,' she murmured inadequately.

Adam breathed deeply, turning away, obviously finding it difficult to retain his composure. 'Where have you been?' he asked tautly.

Maria bit her lip. 'I – I went sightseeing. I – I didn't think you'd miss me.'

'What's that supposed to mean?' he swung round grimly.

She shivered. 'N – nothing. But – well, I thought you'd be working—'

'You're deliberately trying to antagonize me!' he bit out fiercely. 'Just because I've been a little hard on you, mainly I might add because of the cavalier way you've acted, you think you can try and get your own back, is that it?'

'No!' Maria was indignant. 'Oh, it wasn't like that!'

'Then what was it like? What kind of a fool do you think I am? You disappear for more than five hours and expect me to treat you gently! This is London, Maria, not Kilcarney! It can be dangerous for a young inexperienced girl like yourself, unused to the ways of a place like this. Can't you understand that?'

His anger, coming on the heels of that awful confrontation with the policeman, was too much for Maria, and with trembling fingers she covered her eyes and turned away, unwilling to allow him to see her humiliation.

With an impatient exclamation Adam strode across to her, swinging her round to face him. He stared in exasperation at the tears that stained her cheeks, and then heaved a sigh.

'All right, all right,' he said huskily, 'I'm sorry. I'm a

cruel swine, I know, but you nearly scared me out of my wits disappearing like that!'

Maria's lower lip trembled. 'It's been a terrible day,' she said miserably, 'terrible! First there was your anger at breakfast, and then that affair with Miss Griffiths, and then – and then – just now—'

Adam's brows drew together. 'Just now ... what?'

Maria swallowed hard. 'I – I was in the park, I think it was Hyde Park, and this woman spoke to me. I thought she was just being friendly. She asked me a lot of questions about myself, and she seemed genuinely interested. But then this policeman came and shifted her, and told me that she – that she—' She faltered.

Adam pressed his lips together tightly. 'You needn't go on,' he muttered grimly. 'Dear God, Maria, have you no sense?'

Maria sniffed, rubbing her cheeks with her fingers, leaving dirty smudges upon them. 'A – apparently not,' she murmured chokily.

'Oh, Maria!' Adam shook his head wearily. 'Whatever am I going to do with you?' He put up a hand and pushed back a strand of silky hair that was brushing her eye. 'I suppose I'm to blame, really. I haven't exactly tried to understand your reasons for coming here.'

Maria looked appealingly at him. 'I didn't mean to be a nuisance, Adam. I thought – and your mother thought so, too – that you might be glad of my company sometimes.'

Adam's lips drew in rather wryly. 'Yes, I can believe my mother is behind all this,' he commented. 'I'm just surprised your father agreed.'

'My father likes you. He trusts you. He thought I

would be safe with you.'

Adam shook his head. 'What you all seem to over-look is the fact that my work leaves me very little time to be sociable with anyone.'

'Except Loren Griffiths,' murmured Maria bitterly, almost under her breath, but Adam heard and his jaw tightened.

'I don't intend to discuss my affairs with you,' he said sharply. 'Nor do I need your opinion, remember that. But for now, let's try and salvage something from the mess. Have you had anything to eat since you left here?'

'I had some coffee and a doughnut about six o'clock,' she said.

'And are you hungry?'

'Not very.'

Adam studied her, not without resignation. Then he shrugged. 'Mrs. Lacey has left to see her sister this evening. I'm afraid if you do want anything to eat you'll have to trust to my not very adequate culinary practices.'

Maria raised her eyebrows. 'I can cook,' she said quietly.

Adam inclined his head with assumed deference. 'Is that so? Then perhaps you would like to prepare us both some supper.'

Maria's eyes widened. 'You're hungry, too?'

Adam looked sardonic. 'Well, as I had only a salad, and that about five-thirty as Mrs. Lacey wanted to be away early, I guess I could use something.'

Maria tried to smile. 'You would really like me to make you something?'

'Why not? We have the place to ourselves.'

'Are you – I mean – will you be going out again?'

56

Adam hesitated, and then lifted his shoulders. 'Let's hope not,' he commented dryly, and Maria hoped so, too, fervently.

Later, sitting with him at the breakfast bar, eating the prawn omelettes and chips she had prepared, Maria felt happier than she had done since leaving Kilcarney. This was the way she had imagined it would be, talking to Adam, sharing his work with him, listening as he related some amusing anecdotes from his hospital days. She wouldn't think about the depressing hours she had spent alone; she wouldn't think about Loren Griffiths; she would just take every minute as it came and enjoy it.

CHAPTER FOUR

THE following morning Maria overslept, and it was after nine before the penetrating rays of the sun coming through the lemon curtains caused her to open her eyes. She lay for a few moments pleasurably remembering the events of the night before and then slid agilely out of bed.

When she was washed and dressed she went downstairs, going to the kitchen where she could hear the sound of Mrs. Lacey's transistor radio.

'Oh, you're awake at last,' observed the housekeeper smilingly. 'The doctor said not to disturb you.'

'Did he?' Maria made a moue with her lips, wondering whether Adam's motives for saying such a thing were as innocent as they seemed. Then she decided to be charitable, and said: 'It's a marvellous day, isn't it?'

Mrs. Lacey nodded, turning down the radio. 'Yes, beautiful. How would you like me to serve your breakfast on the patio?'

Maria smiled. 'Well, I just want some coffee, that's all. But the patio sounds interesting.'

'Good.' Mrs. Lacey plugged in the percolator, and Maria opened the back door and stepped out into the garden. It was amazing to realize really that they were in the heart of London. It was very quiet, the trees a mass of greenery providing avenues of shade.

After breakfast, Maria came back into the kitchen, biting her lips thoughtfully. 'Did – did Adam say what he expected me to do today?' she asked. 'I mean – I've been here two days now and I'm not used to such an aimless existence. At home there was always plenty to do.'

Mrs. Lacey frowned. 'Well, miss, the doctor said nothing to me, except that I wasn't to allow you to go far alone.'

Maria coloured. 'Oh, did he?'

'Yes, miss. You gave him quite an anxious few hours yesterday, and it's only natural—'

Maria's Irish temper simmered a little. 'What happened yesterday could have happened to anyone!' she averred angrily. 'After all, what would you have done if someone spoke to you in the park?'

'Was that what happened, miss?'

'I thought you knew.'

'Not exactly, miss. The doctor just said you'd had an encounter with the seamier side of London, and that you weren't used to such a big city.'

Maria tossed her head. 'Dublin's not a village, you know!' she exclaimed.

Mrs. Lacey bent her head, refusing to be drawn. 'No, miss,' she replied politely, and Maria turned away impatiently.

'Well, what does he expect me to do?' she cried. 'Is he coming home for lunch today?'

'He didn't say he wasn't, miss.'

'All right. Then I'll sunbathe!'

Maria flounced up to her bedroom, seething with indignation. She felt childlike and irresponsible, and her earlier feeling of contentment had fled. What had last night been, after all? An attempt to placate her and calm her ruffled feelings? She had thought he had enjoyed her company, but now she couldn't be certain. Maybe he had felt guilty at neglecting her, maybe he had been alarmed when she disappeared yesterday, particularly as his mother, as well as her father, expected him to look after her. But even so, if he imagined that treating her as he would treat a child would be satisfactory he was mistaken. She had not come to London to find herself more restricted than she had been back home. She had best make arrangements as soon as possible to take the commercial course, and by so doing remove herself from his authority. When he came home for lunch, she would tackle him on the matter.

Opening a drawer, she extracted a bikini and regarded it critically. Geraldine had bought it for her in one of the big stores in Limerick, knowing her father would never allow her to wear such a thing in Kilcarney. But they had laughed together over it and when Maria was packing to leave she had stuffed it into her suitcase. Now she felt in a mood of rebellion, and the bikini was just the thing to assert her independence.

When she passed through the kitchen on her way to the garden, Mrs. Lacey raised scandalized eyebrows. 'Miss Maria! What are you doing?'

Maria pretended not to understand. 'What do you mean, Mrs. Lacey?' She looked down at the white swimsuit. 'Don't you like it?'

The housekeeper sighed. 'It's very nice, miss, but hardly the thing for a back garden, don't you think?'

Maria shrugged. 'Will the neighbours object?'

Mrs. Lacey wiped her hands on her apron. 'That's not the point, and you know it, miss. After yesterday, I should have thought—'

Maria stiffened. 'Oh, yes? What would you have thought? That perhaps I'm just an innocent abroad!'

'Miss Maria, this is a doctor's household. Can't you think of what Mr. Adam will say?'

Maria raised her eyebrows. 'Don't you think he'll like it?'

'I'm sure he won't.'

'Then – *good*!' Maria wrinkled her nose at the older woman and walked gracefully outside.

Mrs. Lacey stared after her with a worried expression marring her amiable features. She was firmly convinced now that Mr. Adam had taken on more than he had bargained for.

The sound of the doorbell brought Mrs. Lacey round to stare towards the kitchen door doubtfully, and Maria appeared at the back door, her eyes sparkling mischievously. 'Do you think that's Miss Griffiths again?' she asked cheekily.

Mrs. Lacey refused to answer, and leaving her she went to the door. Maria stood listening for a moment, and then hearing the sound of a male voice disappeared outside again. It obviously was not Loren Griffiths, which was a pity.

She stretched out on the garden lounger she had placed strategically in the glare of the sun, and closing her eyes slid dark glasses on to her nose. Presently there was the sound of voices approaching, and her eyes flickered open curiously. Surely the voices were coming towards her?

Sure enough, as she looked towards the rose-coloured trellis that sheltered the arbour where she was sitting, she saw Mrs. Lacey with a man – a young man. Sliding the glasses down her nose, she looked expectantly at the housekeeper before looking back at the young man.

He was very attractive, with curly brown hair, and a strong, muscular body. He was dressed in a patterned shirt with a matching tie, and close-fitting brown trousers. He looked cool and relaxed, and he was regarding Maria with undisguised interest.

Mrs. Lacey stared at Maria disapprovingly, then she said: 'This is the son of one of Mr. Adam's partners, miss, Mr. Larry Hadley.'

Maria slid her legs to the ground and looked across at them smilingly, cradling her sunglasses in her hands. 'Hello,' she said politely. 'Have you come to see Adam?'

'No.' Larry Hadley shook his head. 'I – er – I was in the clinic, seeing Dad this morning, when Adam was talking about you. He seemed to think you might be lonely, so I offered to come round and ... well ...' he moved rather awkwardly ... 'offer my services, as it were.'

Maria glanced at Mrs. Lacey, and then spread her hands. 'That was kind of you. Won't you sit down? I'm sure Mrs. Lacey will provide us with some coffee, won't you, Mrs. Lacey?'

Mrs. Lacey sighed. 'Aren't you going to get changed, miss?'

Maria lifted her shoulders. 'Presently, Mrs. Lacey.'

The housekeeper hovered uncertainly beside them for a moment and then turned and marched into the house. Maria smiled rather apologetically at Larry Hadley, and said: 'Get yourself a lounger from the shed! I'm afraid Mrs. Lacey considers my bikini rather uncircumspect, so don't imagine her rather strained cordiality is on your account.'

Larry Hadley grinned and went to get a lounger,

placing it opposite hers. Then he said: 'Adam says you're here to take a commercial course.'

Maria nodded. 'That's the idea, although as yet I've made no real plans.'

Larry stretched his legs. 'Actually, though, I didn't know Adam had a sister. Until this morning, that is.'

Maria fingered the stems of her sunglasses. 'He hasn't. At least, I'm his stepsister. His mother married my father.'

'I see. Of course, I remember now. But that was before Adam went into partnership with Dad and naturally I forgot.'

Maria studied him curiously. 'What do you do? Do you want to be a doctor, too?'

'Hell, no!' Larry was very definite. 'It's not my idea of a decent job. At present I'm just down from Cambridge. I haven't decided where to direct my talents yet.'

Maria considered this statement thoughtfully. 'You mean you have no occupation?'

'That's right. Oh, I guess I'll have to find something, but I'm not naturally one of the world's workers. I like this kind of existence – relaxed and enjoying the day for what it is, not for what I can get out of it.'

Maria looked a little sceptical. 'That sounds all right in theory,' she commented, 'but it's a little boring in practice, don't you think?' She sighed. 'I want to do something. I don't like being idle all the time.'

Larry stretched his arms behind his head. 'I hope you're not one of the ghastly females who support Women's Liberation, and all that sort of thing!' he exclaimed.

Maria shrugged. 'Not really. Although, I admit, I think women have for years subjugated themselves to the demands of men because they thought that was their only outlet. I believe women are just as intelligent as men, if they apply themselves.'

Larry chuckled. 'Oh, well, so long as they're decorative, too, I shan't object.'

Maria smiled, and Mrs. Lacey returned with the tray of coffee. She made no comment, however, except to ask if they had everything they wanted, and Maria controlled her expression, not wanting to upset the housekeeper any further.

It was pleasant, just sitting there, drinking coffee and talking, and the morning sped away. It was not until they heard the roar of a car engine that Maria realized that this must be Adam, home for lunch.

Larry got to his feet. 'I guess that's your stepbrother,' he said, smoothing a hand over his curly hair. 'Look, I've got to go now, but how about coming out with me this evening? I've got transport. We could go out towards Maidenhead. There's a roadhouse there that serves a jolly good steak.'

Maria hesitated, and then nodded. 'Why not?' she agreed, standing up too. 'I don't suppose Adam has made any plans for me.'

Larry grinned. 'Good! Great! Well, I guess I'd better go . . .'

Even as he spoke, Adam emerged from the house and came striding across the lawns towards them, his face grim. He looked briefly at Larry, returning the younger man's greeting, but his eyes were on Maria, and they were not friendly.

But Maria was unperturbed. If he hadn't wanted Larry to stay so long, he shouldn't have sent him round at all.

'Have you had a good morning?' she asked, stepping

across the grass accompanying Larry to the path which led round the side of the house. 'Larry was just leaving.' They had got on to Christian name terms almost at once.

Adam looked at her intently as she passed him, and said: 'Good-bye, Larry,' in a controlled voice.

Larry smiled, almost apologetically Maria thought, but he winked at her and added: 'I'll call for you about seven, okay?'

'Fine.'

Maria nodded, and the young man walked away to where his car was waiting, just outside the drive gates. Maria turned back and noticed that Adam was still standing in the centre of the lawn, watching her. His hands were thrust deep into his trousers pockets, and his expression was anything but encouraging.

'I think I'll go and change before lunch,' she began, but he took a step forward and said:

'Just a moment, Maria, I want a word with you. *Now!*'

His tone was ominous, and Maria hesitated. 'Can't it wait until I've changed, Adam?'

'No.' Adam extracted a cigar from a case in his pocket, lit it and inhaled deeply before going on: 'Tell me, is your father aware that you possess such a – garment as that?' He flicked a careless hand in the direction of the bikini.

Maria felt herself colouring, and she deliberately pushed her sunglasses on to her nose to give herself the advantage of being able to disguise her expression. 'He knows I have it . . . yes!' she replied defiantly, wishing she had thought to bring down a beach robe as well. Adam's derision was withering.

'I see.' Adam frowned broodingly. 'You amaze me!

However, I'm convinced he wouldn't approve it for wear anywhere but on the beach!'

Maria pressed her lips together. 'All right, all right. Is that all you have to say?'

'No, dammit, it is not.' Adam's voice was heated now. 'Take those damned glasses off. I will not talk to a smoke screen!'

Sighing, Maria drew off the offending glasses, and tried to maintain her composure. She would not allow him to have it all his own way. If he chose to be difficult, then she could be difficult, too.

Adam took his cigar out of his mouth, and studied the glowing tip ill-temperedly. 'What was that young pup doing here?' he demanded harshly.

Maria's eyes widened. 'Young pup? You mean Larry?'

'How many men have you entertained in that get-up?'

Maria clenched her fists at his sarcasm, and said, with as much coolness as she could muster: 'You should know. You sent him.'

'Me?' Adam was forced to stare at her angrily. 'I did no such thing. Did he say I had?'

Maria put a hand to her temple and tried to think. 'I – well – I don't think those were his exact words, but that was what the implication was.'

'Indeed?' Adam sounded sceptical.

'Yes, indeed.' Maria stiffened her shoulders. 'I am not in the habit of lying, if you are.'

'What the hell do you mean?'

Maria coloured. 'Oh, nothing! But there is such a thing as deception, and you seem quite adept at that!'

Adam stared at her. 'Go on!' he said, with controlled

vehemence. 'Go on – who am I deceiving?'

'Well ... well ... your mother, for one,' retorted Maria, rather lamely.

Adam shook his head frowningly. 'Exactly how am I deceiving my mother?'

Maria pressed her hands together. 'You said yourself she didn't know you were engaged.'

Adam gave an exasperated exclamation. 'Oh, for heaven's sake! If you imagine my mother doesn't know about Loren, then you're mistaken. She simply chooses to disregard our relationship.'

Maria clenched her fists. 'I can believe that!'

Adam caught her wrist. 'Now what was that supposed to mean?'

'Nothing.' Maria flushed, wishing she could control her tongue.

Adam chewed at his lower lip. 'As I said before, Maria, I do not intend to listen to your opinions about my affairs.' He thrust her away from him. 'Don't try to justify your own actions by incriminating me.'

Maria heaved a sigh. 'I'm not trying to incriminate anybody. I just object to being treated so off-handedly. I may not have had much freedom at home, but at least I was treated as an adult. I thought last night you were human – but obviously I was mistaken.'

'Last night you deserved a damn sight more than you got. Getting involved with undesirables the minute you're out of my sight!' He raked a hand through his hair. 'A two-year-old would have more sense!'

'How – how dare you speak to me like this! If – if your mother knew—'

'If my mother knew you'd be on the next flight back to the potato fields,' snapped Adam cruelly.

Maria gasped. 'You – you brute!' she cried, and

without really considering her actions, she brought her hand up sharply against his cheek.

Adam stepped back in amazement, and Maria took the chance to escape, rushing into the house as fast as her legs would carry her. In her room she flung herself on the bed, and the tears she had so far suppressed would be denied no longer.

An hour later, when she was still lying face pressed down against the bedspread, there was a knock at her door. 'Go away!' she called in muffled tones, but the door opened and Mrs. Lacey came in carrying a tray.

'Now what's all this?' she asked cajolingly. 'Making yourself ill with crying! I've brought you some lunch. Eat this, and you'll feel better.'

'I don't want anything.' Maria didn't look up, but Mrs. Lacey placed a sympathetic hand on her shoulder.

'Now, child,' she said gently. 'It's no use going on like this. You're making your face all puffy, and I thought I heard you tell that young man you'd go out with him this evening.'

Maria sniffed, and with reluctance pushed herself up on her elbows. 'Oh, Mrs. Lacey,' she said chokingly, 'I slapped him. I slapped Adam!'

'Don't I know it?' Mrs. Lacey hid a smile. 'Made a mess of his face, you did, not to mention his temper!'

Maria sat up properly. 'He'll never forgive me, you know. I don't know what made me to it. We always used to get along so well together. When he came to Ireland, that is. He was very impatient with me, but there was really no need to . . .' She sighed heavily. 'I don't know what came over me. I've always thought of Adam as being a kind of big brother, and I thought he'd be pleased that I wanted to come and stay with him. But he's not . . . he's not!'

Mrs. Lacey clicked her tongue. 'Now, don't go jumping to conclusions, Maria. You don't really know much about your stepbrother yet. He can be the most understanding of men; you should just talk to his patients!'

'Perhaps I should be one of them then,' remarked Maria unhappily. She glanced fearfully towards the open door. 'Where – where is he now?'

'He had a lecture at the hospital this afternoon. You know the sort of thing. Extra-mural activities, and so on.'

Maria put a hand to her mouth. 'But – but what about his face?'

Mrs. Lacey shrugged. 'Yes, I wondered about that, too. No doubt he'll think of something.'

Maria shook her head. 'I really hated him, you know.'

'No, you didn't. You only thought you did,' retorted Mrs. Lacey sharply. 'But I can't say I'm surprised at his reactions to this bikini. Why ever did you decide to wear it?'

Maria sniffed. 'I just wanted to prove to myself that I was independent,' she said. 'In any case, the bikini wasn't really what he was angry about. It was to do with Larry Hadley.'

'Ah, yes,' Mrs. Lacey nodded. 'I wondered whether he'd really asked that young man to come round.'

'But why? I liked Larry. I thought he was nice.'

Mrs. Lacey frowned. 'Well, it has to do with other things,' she said awkwardly. 'And I don't think it's up to me to talk about it. As you say, Larry seems a nice enough young man. Are you going out with him this evening?'

'I said I would. Does – does Adam know?'

'I'm not sure. Anyway, doubtless you'll see him before you go out.'

But as it happened, Maria did not see Adam before she went out. He telephoned Mrs. Lacey around four-thirty to say that he was going straight to the surgery, and as she had no calls for him there was no reason for him to come back. He didn't mention Maria, nor did he ask to speak to her, and she hesitated a long while after this, wondering whether she should telephone Larry and postpone their date.

But in spite of her misgivings, she decided to go. After all, if Adam returned after surgery, the evening would stretch long and uncomfortable before her, and she had no doubt that Adam would in many ways be glad to see the back of her for a while.

So she bathed and changed into a long dress of amber-coloured velvet, that brought out the highlights in her chestnut hair. She did not need a coat, for it was a warm evening, but she took a stole of soft brown wool to put across her arms.

Larry was punctual, bringing his car up the drive this time so that she could walk out and step into it. Mrs. Lacey saw her off, and if she didn't exactly look disapproving, there was an anxious expression on her lined face.

Larry was enthusiastic about her appearance, complimenting her on her dress and generally restoring the confidence that Adam had so badly shaken this morning. They went to the roadhouse he had mentioned and ate steaks and salad, and danced to the beat music that issued from a four-piece group in the corner. As the evening wore on, Maria began to enjoy herself thoroughly, managing to put all thoughts of her stepbrother out of her mind. Larry was a good companion, and although she had had little experience with boys, she knew enough to know when to call a halt.

He drove her home about eleven-thirty. He had wanted to stay later, but Maria was conscious of the fact that this was her first outing with him, and she had no intention of giving Adam more reason to complain.

Even so, she entered the house with some trepidation as Larry drove away, and was almost disappointed when she found there was no one waiting for her. A note from Mrs. Lacey was propped on the mantelshelf in the lounge, but when Maria read it she found it was addressed to Adam, and not herself.

With a strangely depressed feeling, she went to bed.

Next morning, Maria got up early, determining to speak to Adam before he left for the surgery. She purposely dressed in a plain white pleated skirt and a red shirt, not wanting to arouse any more antipathy towards her clothes. She was downstairs by seven-forty-five, and was sitting pretending to read the morning paper in the dining-room when he came in.

She looked up at him warily, conscious that she was becoming intensely aware of him. In a dark suit and a cream shirt and tie, he looked disturbingly attractive, his harsh features possessing a strength of character that was more powerfully devastating than mere good looks could ever be. He looked at Maria with obvious surprise, but took his seat opposite her, responding to her murmured: 'Good morning' with controlled indifference.

Maria sighed, and put the newspaper aside, deciding she might just as well start now as later. 'I want to talk to you, Adam,' she began, in a rather taut voice.

Adam, who had been on the point of reaching for the newspaper she had discarded, frowned. 'Oh, yes?'

'Yes.'

Maria rubbed her hands together on her lap, hiding their nervousness from him. There was no sign now of the livid marks she had made on his face, and she wondered whether it had disappeared so completely from his memory. She doubted it. She might have been sitting opposite a stranger, and she wondered how such a circumstance had come about. Searching for words to begin, she saw an expression of impatience cross his face, and he lifted the newspaper, and scanned its headlines.

Mrs. Lacey came through with his cereal, and she smiled at Maria. Adam thanked her, and began his breakfast, while Maria refused anything but toast as usual. However, Mrs. Lacey did put the percolator beside Maria and she took charge of it with reluctance.

'Do – do you take cream and sugar?' she ventured, as Mrs. Lacey disappeared to get his second course.

Adam looked up. 'Just sugar, thank you,' he replied bleakly, and Maria added two lumps and passed him the cup. He took it from her, placing it on the table, and continued to study his newspaper.

'Oh, for goodness' sake!' Maria felt angry. 'Haven't you anything to say to me?'

Adam looked at her coldly. 'I understood you had

something to say to me.'

Maria sighed. 'I did. I do! But – about yester-day—'

'I think we'll forget what happened yesterday.'

Maria tugged at a strand of her hair. 'But you haven't. Oh, Adam, we can't go on like this, arguing all the time.'

'I agree.'

She pressed her lips together. 'Do – do you expect me to say I'll leave?'

Adam shrugged. 'I would not be so optimistic,' he remarked sarcastically, and she had to concentrate hard not to make some retaliatory comment.

'Are you going to allow me to stay and take this course, then?'

'Do I have any choice?'

Maria shook her head angrily. 'Oh, stop talking to me like this! You know you have the final word. You have only to write to my father telling him what I've been doing and he'll demand that I return home. Particularly if it was phrased in the way you would phrase it. I know.'

Adam sighed and laid his newspaper aside. 'You must admit, Maria, you've deliberately set out to antagonize me.'

Maria stared at him indignantly. 'No, I haven't!'

'Then why did you wear that bikini yesterday?'

Maria bent her head. In retrospect that seemed rather silly now. 'I don't know,' she said, at last. 'I'd never worn it before, and it seemed a good idea at the time.'

Adam gave an impatient exclamation, and Maria cast a cautious glance in his direction. 'You're an innocent!' he said heavily. 'You've got some crazy idea that because your clothes are sophisticated, you're sophisticated too. Clothes don't do anything but cover you!'

Maria flushed. 'I don't suppose you'd have objected so violently if it had been Loren Griffiths wearing the bikini,' she muttered mutinously.

Adam's expression hardened. 'I'll ignore that remark, Maria.'

Maria tapped her teeth with a fingernail. 'Are you going to send me back to Kilcarney, Adam?' she asked, appealingly.

He shrugged. 'What's so objectionable about Kilcarney?'

Maria sighed. 'You don't know what it's like – how narrow an existence it really is. All people do there is get married, have children, raise them.'

Adam gave her a sardonic look. 'It's a common enough pattern.'

'But not for me!'

'Get to the point, Maria. Why don't you want to go back?'

Maria looked down at the table. 'My father thinks I'm old enough to settle down.'

'Settle down? You mean – get married?'

'Yes.'

Adam frowned. 'I see. And I suppose he has someone in mind.'

'Yes, Matthew Hurley.'

'The name's familiar. I'm not certain, but wasn't that the name of the man whose land marched with your father's? I vaguely recall meeting someone of that name when your father took me down to the inn.'

Maria bent her head. 'That's right. You probably met Matt's father. But he's dead now, he died two years ago, and the farm's Matt's now.'

'Ah!' Adam nodded. 'And your father thinks that if you marry Matthew Hurley, he'll have control of both farms.'

'Something like that.'

'So how did you manage to persuade him to allow you to come to England?'

'I didn't. Geraldine did. She said it wasn't right that a girl of my age should be expected to leave school and immediately plunge into marriage with a man I hardly knew. She said I should have a few months of freedom to decide what I wanted to do, and she persuaded my father to let me come to England to take this course so that I would have qualifications for something apart from childbearing!' She coloured hotly.

'I see. It's typical of my mother, of course, using you for her ends as well as your own.'

Maria sighed. 'I didn't know anything about that. I just know I don't want to go back there and be practically forced to marry Matt.'

'You don't love him, I gather?'

'No!' Maria was adamant. 'He's all right, but there's nothing between us, no spark . . . nothing!'

Adam shook his head. 'I think my mother has filled your head with impractical romantic ideas,' he remarked dryly. 'Being married – having children. They're not things to despise.'

'I don't despise them. I want to get married, I want to have babies!' She coloured again. 'But with the right man, not just the expedient one!'

Adam shrugged and Mrs. Lacey returned with his bacon and eggs. Maria applied herself to buttering a slice of toast and adding some of Mrs. Lacey's delicious home-made marmalade, while Adam tackled his meal.

From time to time she stole a glance at him, wondering what he was thinking now. He had said nothing to make her think that he felt any more tolerably towards her, and yet she sensed that some of the antagonism had dispersed.

By the time he was buttering himself some toast, she could contain herself no longer, and she said awkwardly: 'Are – are you going to write to my father, Adam?'

He handed her his cup and she filled it with coffee before he spoke. Then he regarded her sternly. 'And if I say I'll refrain from doing so, will you refrain from behaving like a schoolgirl on the loose?'

Maria compressed her lips. 'I won't wear the bikini, if that's what you mean.'

'That isn't what I meant, although I guess that's all part of it. It's this childish behaviour every time I try to impose a little discipline. All right, I'll accept that your father has been pretty strict with you in the past, and you're wanting your independence, but I will not condone irresponsible actions; nor will I tolerate them. Do I make myself clear?'

Maria stared down at her plate. She felt as though she was being cleverly blackmailed into a situation which she would regret later. But what could she do? He held all the cards.

'All right,' she said, in a small voice. 'I'll try and do what you say.'

'Good.' Adam wiped his mouth on his napkin and rose from the table. 'Now I must go. Regarding your intention to take a commercial course, would you like me to get Janet to find out about them for you?'

Maria frowned. 'Who is Janet?'

'My receptionist.'

'I see. All right then, if that's what you want.'

Adam controlled his impatience. 'It's what you want, isn't it?'

Maria lifted her shoulders and then let them fall. 'I – I suppose so.'

Adam turned away before he could show his exasperation, and Maria watched him leave the room with some misgivings. She supposed in a way she had won a minor victory, but it was indeed very minor. He had practically forced her to accept his terms, and now he had even taken the opportunity for finding her own way around out of her hands too. Still, perhaps it was just as well, and once she had settled into college life, things would be different.

CHAPTER FIVE

On Saturday morning, at the end of Maria's first week in England, Adam's receptionist telephoned her to say that she had made inquiries on her behalf regarding the commercial courses open to her and she had two suggestions to offer. The first was that Maria should join a class which had been operating since the beginning of the summer term, four weeks ago, and where it was possible to catch up with what had gone before. The second was that she should delay starting at all until after the summer vacation when she would be able to begin with a new class altogether.

Maria took down all the details as she was given them, and thanked the receptionist politely for her trouble. Then she regarded what she had written rather doubtfully. Of course, the second suggestion was easily the most appealing, but somehow she did not think Adam would agree to that when this other course was already operating and there was no reason why she shouldn't be able to catch up with them.

Sighing, she went into the kitchen to consult Mrs. Lacey and the housekeeper made coffee and they had their usual half hour together. During the past two days she had seen little of Adam, except at mealtimes, and she had come to rely on Mrs. Lacey for conversation. She had not gone further than the High Street since her confrontation with Adam, and she was rapidly becoming restless and bored. Mrs. Lacey would let her do nothing in the house, and Adam seemed to think she had no interest in his affairs. She would have loved to have visited his clinic and met some of his patients, but it seemed as though he was determined to keep her out of his life as much as he could.

She had never done so much reading in her life before, and sometimes she played records on the stereo, although some of Adam's records did not appeal to her. However, she found that the more she listened to them, the more she liked and understood them, and when she found books in Adam's shelves about their composers, she read those, too.

And yet, for all that, she still had no desire to return to Ireland, and with eternal optimism assured herself that sooner or later things would improve.

Mrs. Lacey had no constructive suggestions to offer concerning commercial courses, and her usual edict was that Maria should consult Adam.

'But he never has time to talk to me!' Maria protested. 'He always seems to be called away just as we're in the middle of a conversation.'

'A doctor's life is not ruled by schedules,' replied Mrs. Lacey, sipping coffee. 'He's constantly at the mercy of his patients.'

'I know.' Maria cupped her chin with one hand.

'Well, anyway,' confided Mrs. Lacey reassuringly, 'as from lunchtime today it's Mr. Adam's week-end off, and someone else will take all his calls for him.'

Maria stared at her. 'Is that so?'

'Of course. You don't suppose someone can work twenty-four hours a day, seven days a week, without a break, do you?'

Maria lifted her shoulders in anticipation. 'I didn't really think about it. That's marvellous! Now we'll have a chance—'

'Now hold on!' Mrs. Lacey's tone was dampening.

'You're forgetting – your stepbrother has other commitments apart from his work.'

Maria's shoulders sagged. 'You mean Loren Griffiths, don't you?'

Mrs. Lacey shrugged. 'Partly.'

Maria pressed her lips together. 'How – how long has Adam known her?'

'Miss Griffiths?' Mrs. Lacey frowned. 'About eighteen months – or two years perhaps. I can't be certain. Why?'

Maria made an indifferent gesture. 'Curiosity, that's all.' She frowned. 'Does he – love her?'

'Well, I suppose he must, mustn't he? Seeing as he's engaged to her and all.'

'When – when will they get married?'

Mrs. Lacey carried her cup across to the draining board. 'Your guess is as good as mine. I suppose she would like him to give up this practice and join one of those Harley Street clinics, where all the rich people go.'

Maria stared at the housekeeper's back. 'And will Adam do that?'

'Who knows? I should say no, if I were asked, but you never can tell. If he loves her enough, he'll do it, I suppose.'

Maria stared down at the patterned surface of the breakfast bar, feeling suddenly very disturbed. In her mind's eye she could see Adam very clearly as she had seen him last evening at dinner. For all she found his dictates harsh, she admired him tremendously for what he was doing, and to imagine him giving it all up for that decorative doll of an actress made her feel slightly sick. She could understand why Loren Griffiths found him so attractive, but it was the very qualities that

Loren would like to destroy that made him the man he was. A vivid picture of them together, Loren's soft arms wrapped round him possessively, her whole body straining towards him, caused Maria to utter a bitter deprecation of her imagination, and she slid jerkily off her stool and walked quickly out of the room.

Adam telephoned about eleven to say he would not be in to lunch after all, and Maria came rushing down the stairs from her room as Mrs. Lacey was replacing the receiver.

'He's not coming home for lunch?' she exclaimed dejectedly.

'No.'

'Well, where is he going? I thought you said he was finished after lunch today.'

'So he is. I imagine he's taking lunch with Miss Griffiths.'

'Oh – oh, *blast!*'

Maria sank down on to the bottom stair, resting her chin on her fists unhappily. She had been planning what she was going to say to him when he came home, and now he wasn't coming.

Mrs. Lacey sighed. 'Now, miss, this is silly. You've surely learned by now that you can't expect to make demands on Mr. Adam's time. He has so little free time, when all's said and done. It's natural he should want – well, feminine companionship.'

Maria looked up broodingly. 'Am I not feminine, then?'

'Now you know what I mean, miss.'

'Yes, I know,' muttered Maria glumly. 'Oh, Mrs. Lacey, whatever am I going to do all day?'

'Well, I'm going to see my sister this afternoon, miss. Mr. Adam always gives me Saturday afternoons and evenings off, and I go over to Elsie's and we go and have a game of bingo at the club. If I were you, I'd find myself a nice book and sit in the garden this afternoon. Mr. Adam always comes back around five to change, whatever his plans, and you'll see him then.'

Maria digested this. 'All right, all right,' she said, feeling depressed. 'I suppose I'll just entertain myself as usual.' She sighed. 'I'm surprised Larry Hadley hasn't phoned, though. He said he would. You haven't taken any calls for me while I've been out shopping, have you, Mrs. Lacey?'

Mrs. Lacey looked rather uncomfortable suddenly. Turning away, she said: 'I really must go and get on with lunch. We have to eat, even if Mr. Adam isn't coming in.'

Maria stood up, frowning. 'You didn't answer me, Mrs. Lacey. Have there been any calls? Did you forget to tell me?'

Mrs. Lacey shook her head. 'As if I'd forget, miss,' she prevaricated. 'Now, if you'll excuse me—'

'No, wait!' Maria walked round the housekeeper so that she could read her expression. 'Mrs. Lacey, are you telling me the truth?'

Mrs. Lacey heaved a sigh, pleating and unpleating her apron with restless fingers. 'Well, miss, if you must know, the doctor said that if Mr. Hadley should ring you, I was to say you were not available.'

'What!' Maria was flabbergasted. 'How dare he do such a thing? And why? Because of my date with him the other evening?'

Mrs. Lacey shook her head. 'No, miss. Mr. Adam doesn't know about that.'

'He doesn't know?' Maria stared at the housekeeper. 'But – he must do!'

'No, miss. If you remember, he was out when you went out, and you came home before he did. Then the next morning he told me not to accept any calls from Mr. Hadley for you, and I didn't like to tell him then that you'd been out with the young man the night before.'

'Oh, lord!' Maria swept a hand through her hair. 'And what reason has he for trying to prevent me seeing Larry?'

'I'd rather not say, miss.'

'Come on! This is ridiculous, Mrs. Lacey.'

'Well, maybe it is, and maybe it isn't. Either way, it's nothing to do with me, miss. I don't gossip about things like that.'

Maria gave her an exasperated look. 'Well, anyway, has Larry phoned?'

Mrs. Lacey shrugged. 'I don't know that I ought to tell you.' Then she sighed. 'Oh, very well, yes, he has – twice.'

'Twice!' Maria gasped. 'Honestly, this is worse than being at home. I – I shall speak to Adam when he comes in.'

'I shouldn't, miss. It will only cause more trouble—'

'Trouble! *Trouble!*' cried Maria tremulously. 'He doesn't know the meaning of the word – yet!'

Mrs. Lacey went out soon after two o'clock. Maria watched her ample bulk amble down the drive and disappear in the direction of the bus stop, and then she walked into the hall and picked up the telephone. Half an hour later Larry Hadley arrived, walking confidently into the hall when Maria opened the door. 'Hi,' he said, grinning. 'I thought I'd offended you or something, from the chilly refusals I've had from your housekeeper.'

Maria smiled in return. 'Oh, it was just a mix-up over phone calls,' she explained charmingly. 'It was lucky you were in when I rang just now.'

'Yes, it was,' Larry nodded, surveying the attractive picture she made in slim-fitting cream trousers and a scarlet shirt with some pleasure. 'I was just getting ready to go over to the tennis club, actually, and I wondered whether that might appeal to you, too. Do you play?'

Maria looked enthusiastic. 'Yes, of course,' she said. 'But I'm afraid I don't have a racket with me.'

'Never mind. You can borrow one at the club. Do you want to go then?'

'I'd love to. Just hang on a moment while I change into something more suitable.'

'Okay.'

Larry strolled into the lounge, and Maria ran hastily upstairs. In no time she had stripped off the red shirt and the cream trousers and had donned a short-skirted white tunic that she usually wore with a coloured sash to give it distinction. But without the sash, it was just the thing for such an energetic game as tennis, and when she came downstairs Larry whistled his approval.

'Nice,' he said, hands in his pockets. 'You'll create quite a sensation down at the club. It's seldom we see any completely new faces.'

The Blakeley Tennis Club was quite an exclusive establishment, catering mainly for the youth of the professional families in the area. Maria had never been to such a place, but happily she was accepted as Adam Massey's stepsister, and her youth and natural exuberance attracted quite a lot of attention from the male members. It was easy to hire a racket for the afternoon, and Maria's first game was a singles match with Larry.

Conscious of the eyes of their spectators, Maria played badly and Larry won easily, but later, when she partnered him against another young couple, they won, and he took her into the clubhouse to buy her a congratulatory drink.

She was introduced to dozens of people, but names just drifted over her head, and the only couple she really got to know were Evelyn James and David Hallam. Evelyn was the daughter of a bank manager, while David's father was a solicitor. Maria liked David, he was good fun, and later, when he asked if he might take her out that evening, she wanted to accept. But she had been aware of Evelyn's jealous gaze ever since David started showing a developing interest in her, and besides, there was Larry to consider. So she refused, and David informed her in a low tone that he would phone her at the beginning of the following week.

As it was quite late, Larry suggested that they ought to be making for home, and once in the car he said:

'What were you and David talking about so earnestly?'

Maria shrugged. 'This and that,' she temporized.

'He's interested in you, isn't he?' Larry sounded annoyed. 'It's a bit much!'

'What is?' Maria looked at him innocently.

'Playing one of us off against the other.'

'Don't be silly. I wasn't doing that. If you must know David asked me out this evening, and I refused.'

'Oh!' Larry was silent for a moment. 'I'm sorry, Maria. I guess I'm just jealous, that's all. Say, how about you and me going to a show this evening? We could have a snack beforehand, and then have supper afterwards.'

Maria hesitated. 'I don't know, Larry,' she began doubtfully. 'I don't know what Adam is doing, you see.'

Larry sighed. 'Well, hell, he doesn't seem to care what you do.'

'Doesn't he? I wonder.' Maria sounded uncertain. 'Look, Larry, let's leave it for tonight. Give me a ring tomorrow some time, if you want to.'

Larry was disgruntled, but there was nothing he could do, and he dropped her at the foot of Adam's drive and drove away rather fiercely, revving his engine with a childish show of power.

Maria walked slowly up the drive; Adam's car was parked to one side of the house, and she was in no hurry to begin the arguments that were bound to ensue. She entered the hall quietly, and closed the door with stealthy movements.

Then she waited, listening, wondering where he was and what he was doing. There was no sound from anywhere, and she pressed her lips together and walked to the door of the lounge. The room was deserted, as was the kitchen and the dining-room. She frowned. He must be upstairs getting changed. Mrs. Lacey had said he came back to change. With a sigh, Maria entered the lounge, flinging herself down on to the couch, and kicking off her plimsolls. It was pleasant to wriggle her toes, and she was doing just that when a sound made her look up. Adam was standing in the doorway, sleek and sophisticated in a dark blue suit, and a pale blue shirt and tie.

'You're back!' he observed coolly. 'Exactly where have you been?'

Maria stretched back on the couch, determined not to let him intimidate her. 'I've been to the tennis club – with Larry.'

'Hadley?'

'Yes.'

Adam frowned. 'I see. Did he come round?'

'No, I rang him up and asked him to take me out.'

'You did what!' Adam was astounded.

'I rang him up and asked him to take me out,' she repeated calmly, more calmly than she felt. 'Mrs. Lacey told me you had commanded that he shouldn't be allowed to speak to me, so I decided I would speak to him!'

Adam made no reply to this impudence, but walked slowly into the room, taking up a stance near her, towering over her as she lay, feeling wholly vulnerable now, on the couch. 'I see,' he remarked expressionlessly.

Maria sat up, feeling slightly uncomfortable under his scrutiny. 'Don't worry, Mrs. Lacey didn't betray your confidence willingly. I practically forced a confession out of her.'

'I never doubted Mrs. Lacey's integrity,' he said blandly.

Maria heaved a sigh. 'Well, anyway, I was sick of being on my own. I wanted someone to talk to. And Mrs. Lacey was going out.'

'Yes, to her sisters. She goes every week.'

'Yes, she told me.' Maria examined her fingernails. 'And as you were out, too . . .'

Adam raised his dark eyebrows. 'I lunched with Loren.'

Maria compressed her lips. 'And what did you do afterwards?'

He shrugged. 'Very little.'

Maria felt the hot colour rising up her cheeks. 'How nice!' she observed impudently.

Adam put out a hand, catching her chin and lifting her face so that she was forced to look at him. 'What I do is my business,' he said harshly. 'Now, I thought we had an understanding – regarding discipline.'

'Doing as I'm told, you mean!' she snapped, jerking her chin away from him, disturbed by the cool hardness of his touch.

Adam's expression was bleak. 'Doing as I think best,' he amended coldly. 'My reasons for not wanting you to associate with Larry Hadley are valid ones, believe me!'

Maria looked mutinously at him. 'You seem to forget, I spend nine-tenths of my life within these four walls at the moment. I do happen to get bored, you know.'

'Nobody asked you to come,' returned Adam briefly, and Maria hunched her shoulders.

'I think you're determined to make me so unhappy that I'll leave of my own accord, aren't you?'

Adam stared at her. 'I am not. Good lord, didn't Janet just contact you this morning about those commercial courses? If I was attempting to drive you away, I would hardly have my receptionist waste time finding out about necessary courses in shorthand and typewriting!'

Maria heaved a sigh. 'You can't forbid me to have friends!'

'I'm not trying to do so. But as yet you've had very little opportunity to make friends.'

'Whose fault is that?'

Adam thrust his hands into his trousers pockets.

'Mine, I suppose,' he said exasperatedly. 'Oh, Maria, you do create problems!'

'Thank you.' Maria looked miserably down at her knees. Then a thought occurred to her. 'Are – are you going out again?'

Adam raked a hand through his hair. 'I was,' he muttered impatiently.

'Where?' Maria looked up at him, her tawny eyes wide and disappointed.

Adam walked away from her, standing staring through the french doors on to the garden. 'I was going to Fincham, with Loren,' he said resignedly.

'Fincham?' Maria frowned. 'What's that?'

Adam turned, looking at her through the veil of his long lashes which were the only feminine thing about a face that was harshly attractive. 'It's a fishing village in Kent,' he replied. 'Loren has a cottage there.'

Maria stared at him, and then the colour in her cheeks deepened. 'I – I see,' she said, feeling an awful tight feeling in her chest.

Adam bit angrily at his lower lip. 'Well, for God's sake, don't look so disapproving! I've been there before.'

Maria tried to act indifferently. 'I – I'm sure you have,' she responded unevenly. 'It – it looks like being a fine week-end. You should enjoy it.'

Adam uttered an expletive, and strode across to her with some impatience. 'Go and pack a few things,' he said grimly. 'You're coming with me.'

Maria stared at him in horror. 'Oh, no – no, I'm not! I – I wouldn't dream of – of intruding!'

Adam's expression was savage. 'Go and do as you're told, Maria,' he muttered violently, 'or I may be tempted to use other methods to make you obey

89

orders.'

Maria stared at him as a rabbit stares at a snake, and then with an exclamation slid off the couch. 'But – but what will Mrs. Lacey think?' she began.

'I'll leave a message for Mrs. Lacey,' replied Adam, taking a pen out of his pocket. 'Now go!'

Maria ran upstairs, her heart pounding painfully. How could Adam decide to take her to Loren's week-end cottage, just like that? And what would Loren say? She would be absolutely furious, Maria knew. She was just not the kind of woman to permit those kind of liberties. All Maria could look forward to was a week-end acting as an unwanted third between two people who were only interested in each other. The knowledge caused a sudden pain in the pit of her stomach. The last thing she wanted was to have to spend time watching Adam being enslaved by Loren's undoubted allure.

But she had no choice. She could not even make the excuse of already having a date with Larry, for she had turned his offer down. She would simply have to go and try and keep out of their way as much as possible.

When she had changed back into the cream trousers and the red shirt she had been wearing earlier, and had packed some shorts, a couple of dresses and a simple one-piece bathing suit in a small suitcase, she came back downstairs to find Adam still in the lounge, smoking a cigar and studying an article in one of his bulky medical reference books. He looked up as she entered and his gaze flickered over her slacks and shirt with momentary appraisal.

'I – I'm ready,' she said awkwardly. 'Are – are you sure Miss Griffiths won't object?'

Adam's eyes narrowed slightly. 'Leave Miss Griffiths

to me,' he returned smoothly, and thrust the book he was holding back into the bookshelves. 'Are you taking a coat?'

'Just my anorak,' she said quietly, and he nodded.

'Right. Shall we go?'

Maria nodded, and as she turned to leave the room she noticed the note to Mrs. Lacey propped upon the mantelshelf. Outside the Rover 2000 waited for them, Adam's suitcase slung on the back seat. However, he took it out and placed it, together with Maria's, in the boot of the car. Maria hesitated about getting into the front seat beside him, and he said shortly:

'It's all right. You can get into the back after we pick up Loren.'

Maria hunched her shoulders and slid into the front seat, and Adam started the engine. It was the first time she had driven with him and in normal circumstances she would have enjoyed it, but as it was she was apprehensive about Loren Griffiths' reactions and not looking forward at all to witnessing her impatience.

They drove through the busy traffic to Loren's town house and Adam parked at the foot of a flight of steps leading up to the door of a narrow Georgian residence whose lace-curtained windows were made gay with window boxes, and where tubs of hydrangeas brightened the porch. Adam looked across at her and said: 'Will you wait here, or do you want to come with me?'

Maria coloured. 'I'll wait here. I – I'll get into the back while I'm waiting.'

Adam hesitated, looked as though he was about to say something more, and then slid abruptly out of the vehicle. As he mounted the steps, Maria hastily transferred herself and her possessions to the back seat, and watched surreptitiously as he approached the door. To her surprise, he took out a key and let himself into the building, and she sank back into her corner miserably. Her natural antipathy towards Loren was heightened by Adam's casual intimacy with her, and she knew with a sinking feeling of inadequacy that part of her aversion for the other woman was caused by jealousy.

It was almost fifteen minutes before Adam emerged again, now accompanied by Loren Griffiths and an elderly woman. Maria had begun to feel restless and thoughts of getting out of the car and disappearing into the afternoon crowds crossed her mind. And when she saw the expression on Loren's face she wished she had done just that. The other woman looked venomous, and didn't even bother to speak to Maria as Adam helped her into the front beside the driving seat. The elderly woman opened the rear and smiled at Adam as he came to help her in too before casting a doubtful look in Maria's direction. Maria hunched herself into one corner, and wished desperately that she had had some excuse to offer when Adam had suggested this arrangement.

Adam slid into his seat and glancing round, he said: 'Oh, Alice, this is my stepsister Maria. Maria, this is Loren's housekeeper, Alice. She usually accompanies us to Fincham.' The way he said this latter sentence left Maria in no doubt as to his implication, and she managed a polite greeting to Alice, preferring to avoid Adam's mocking gaze.

The drive down to Kent was not as unpleasant as Maria had half dreaded it might be. To begin with, Loren seemed to have chosen to ignore her presence altogether, and so long as she had Adam's undivided attention she didn't seem to care about the others in the back. This left Maria to Alice's speculative appraisal, but after a while, as everyone relaxed, Alice began to talk to her quite kindly, asking her about her life in Ireland, and discussing the position she hoped to obtain after she had acquired some commercial qualifications. Maria decided she liked Alice, even if she was Loren's housekeeper, and pretty soon she was chattering away quite naturally, forgetting that her stepbrother and his fiancée could overhear everything they said.

'Back home we live near the sea,' she was saying, as the road curved and they all glimpsed the wide expanse of water in the distance. 'We're lucky really, we have the benefit of both countryside and seaside.'

Alice nodded interestedly. 'And what brought you to London?' she asked curiously.

Maria smiled. 'Oh, Geraldine talked about it so much I was dying to see it,' she confessed. 'Geraldine is Adam's mother, you know, she married my father.'

'Yes, I know,' Alice nodded again.

'Well, anyway, I thought it would be rather fun, coming to England, and living with Adam.' Maria sighed. 'I think being a doctor is really rather exciting, don't you? I mean – you're dealing with people's lives, aren't you?' She frowned. 'Whenever Adam came to Kilcarney, he used to talk about his work a lot to my father and I used to listen. It always fascinated me, learning about the intricacies of the human body.'

'And didn't you think you might like to be a nurse?'

'Oh, no. I'd get too involved,' said Maria honestly. 'I don't think I'd ever get used to the realization that for some people there is no cure – no happy ending.'

Alice considered her gently. 'And are you enjoying

93

yourself so far?' she inquired. 'Does London live up to your expectations?'

Maria hesitated. 'I suppose so,' she replied cautiously. 'Not that I've seen much of it yet, of course. Next week – next week when I arrange about taking the course, then I might get to see more of it.'

'So you've decided to stay?'

Maria frowned. 'Why, yes.'

Alice shrugged. 'I thought Miss Griffiths said there was some doubt.'

Maria's cheeks burned and she stared hard at the back of Adam's neck. 'No,' she said clearly. 'No, there's no doubt.'

Fincham was not much bigger than a village, but there were some large houses on its outskirts which denoted the prosperity of some of its occupants. It was the ideal spot for Londoners wanting a week-end away from town, and there was a good beach as well as a small marina for yachtsmen.

Adam drove through the village and out at its furthest side and Maria looked out of the car's windows with interest, forgetting momentarily her anger earlier on. It was a lovely evening, the sun turning the sky to molten gold. They followed a narrow track along the cliff edge, and finally curved between the gates of a villa perched high on the cliffs. Maria stared at the whitewashed walls of the building curiously, wondering exactly where Loren Griffiths' cottage might be.

Alice began gathering her belongings together and Maria looked at her expectantly. 'We're here,' said Alice, smiling.

Maria looked again out of the window. 'You mean – you mean – this villa – this is the cottage?'

Now Loren glanced round at her impatiently. 'Of

course it is. What did you expect? A stone-built shack without any water or electricity?'

Maria refrained from making any retort, and as Adam stopped the car she opened her door and slid out.

The sea air was chill after the heat of the car, but it was wonderfully refreshing, too. Where the villa stood they had a magnificent view of the village below them at the foot of the cliffs, and now Maria could see that a flight of steps led down from the villa to the beach below. It was very beautiful and very secluded, and the perfect hideaway for someone like Loren.

Adam climbed out too and glanced at Maria before going to open Loren's door. Maria returned his look defiantly, and saw a flicker of exasperation cross his face, before he said: 'Do you like it?'

Maria shrugged, unwilling to agree with him. 'It's all right,' she replied indifferently, and he moved away to open Loren's door.

Loren got out elegantly, showing the slender curve of her legs. She was wearing a mini dress, a silky soft suede coat overall. The coat was calf length, but she allowed it to swing open to reveal the shorter skirt beneath. She was very petite, and Maria felt huge beside her.

Even as Adam was getting the cases out of the boot the door of the villa opened and a woman appeared. She was wearing a coat and hat and carried a shopping bag. When she saw Loren, she came hurrying over, and Alice, who was beside Maria, explained in an undertone that this was Mrs. Jennings, the daily, who looked after the villa and who prepared the place before Loren arrived.

Mrs. Jennings said that she had left a cold meal

ready for them, and then went on her way, while the others walked up the path to the door, Adam bringing the cases.

They entered into a huge lounge that ran from front to back of the villa, and it was from this room that a staircase curved into the upper regions of the house. It was comfortably if not opulently furnished and there were rafters here as though the house possessed an age that was not evident from outside. To the right of this room, a door opened through to a dining-room, which in turn gave on to a large modern kitchen, and Maria, following Alice through to the kitchen, realized that it was not as big a house as she had at first thought.

The meal was laid in the dining-room and Maria hovered about as Alice shed her coat and put on the kettle. 'Go through to the lounge,' said Alice, at last, frowning at the girl. 'Miss Griffiths won't eat you, you know.'

Maria sighed. 'I wish I could be as certain. She didn't take kindly to my coming, did she?'

Alice gave a rueful smile. 'No, I suppose not, but then she considers your stepbrother her personal and private property, and she hates to have her plans thwarted.'

Maria coloured. 'I see. And is he?'

'Is he what?' Alice frowned.

'Is Adam her property?'

Alice opened her mouth to make some retort and then she gave a brief exclamation, looking beyond Maria to someone who was standing right behind her. Maria swung round, her heart pounding nervously, and confronted Adam who stood in the kitchen doorway supporting himself against the lintel.

He straightened as she looked at him and said:

'Exactly what do you mean by that remark, Maria?'

Maria's cheeks burned. 'I – I – where's Miss Griffiths?'

'Miss Griffiths has gone to her room to change for dinner,' returned Adam coldly. 'Now, come through to the lounge. I want to speak to you.'

Maria hesitated. 'Can't it wait, Adam?' she asked unevenly. 'I – I'm helping Alice.'

'Like hell you are!' Adam controlled his temper with difficulty, a muscle jerking in his cheek. 'Come along. I have a few words to say to you in private!'

CHAPTER SIX

In the lounge Adam faced her angrily. 'Exactly what do you mean by discussing me with Alice?' he exclaimed fiercely.

Maria moved uncomfortably. 'It was something she said that I was questioning,' she defended herself awkwardly.

'I see.' Adam regarded her broodingly. 'And didn't it occur to you not to gossip?'

'Where you're concerned? No.'

'Why?'

'Because you've obviously been talking about me,' she retaliated.

'Oh, have I? What makes you say that?'

'You must have heard what Alice said in the car. She said she thought there was some doubt about my staying here – in England, I mean.'

'What has that got to do with me?'

'Well, you must have said something.'

'What Loren tells her housekeeper is no concern of mine.'

Maria coloured. 'And you deny discussing me with her?'

Adam's eyes narrowed. 'Damn you, I don't have to give an account of myself to you!'

Maria sighed. 'Anyway, it's obvious that she didn't want me to come here, isn't it?'

'I guess so.' Adam raked a hand through his hair. 'However, if I say you're staying, you're staying, is that clear?'

Maria pressed her lips together. 'Perfectly.'

Adam turned away, drawing out his case of cigars. 'You just might enjoy it, have you thought of that?'

'Frankly, no.' Maria was in no mood to be tactful. 'How long are we staying?'

'Until Monday morning. We'll drive back to town in time for lunch.'

'Monday!' Maria was aghast. That meant more than another whole day here. 'Am I – I mean – should I change for dinner, too?'

Adam regarded her slacks and shirt critically. 'Not if you don't want to.'

Maria bent her head. It didn't matter anyway. Loren would be sure to eclipse them all with her delicate face and form. Hunching her shoulders, Maria walked across to the wide windows, looking out on the spectacular view of cliff and sea and skyline. Darkness was drawing in and down in the village the glimmer of lights could be seen. She should have felt pleased and excited at the prospect of a week-end by the sea, but instead she felt nervous and ill at ease, and she wished she could escape from the imminent dinner with Adam and Loren. She would be hopelessly *de trop*, and Adam should have considered this before inviting her.

Now he came to stand beside her, looking down at her with thoughtful eyes. 'It's a magnificent view, isn't it?' he asked, offering her a chance to forget what was past.

Maria nodded. 'Yes. It's not at all what I expected.'

'No, I gathered that. What did you expect? Something like what Loren depicted?'

'Something like that.'

'You should have realized that someone as fastidious

as Loren would hardly settle for anything less than luxury.'

'I suppose I should.' Maria felt disgruntled. 'I thought you would be alone down here. I didn't imagine she would bring her housekeeper along.'

'Oh, yes?' Adam was wary. 'Why?'

Maria's colour deepened. 'It's obvious, isn't it?' she replied, rather imprudently.

Adam swung her round to face him. 'No, it is not obvious, to me, at least,' he snapped. 'If you're thinking what I think you're thinking, then you can forget it! If I want to sleep with Loren, I don't have to drive ninety miles to the Kent coast to accomplish it!'

Maria's cheeks burned, and she struggled to free herself impotently. 'Let me go,' she cried unhappily. 'Oh, I wish you'd never brought me here! I didn't want to come. You know I didn't. I think you're just trying to humiliate me!'

Adam let her go suddenly and the unexpected release sent her stumbling backwards to trip over the low table on the hearth and land in an ignominious heap in the corner by the fireplace. She hit her head as she fell, and for a moment the room spun dizzily.

Immediately Adam was at her side, down on his haunches, helping her to her feet, his hands probing her temple exploringly, his eyes dark and disturbed. 'Are you all right?' he demanded, rather harshly. 'I'm sorry if I caused this. I didn't intend to hurt you.'

Maria quivered under his hands, suddenly weak with emotion, and managed to step back away from him. 'I – I'm fine,' she protested huskily. 'It – it was my fault.'

He surveyed her intently, his eyes probing in their scrutiny. 'It wasn't your fault,' he contradicted softly.

'I was to blame. If I hadn't lost my temper it wouldn't have happened. Look, can't we try and call a truce this week-end? Couldn't we try and enjoy one another's company?'

Maria looked at him tremulously. 'I do enjoy your company,' she murmured honestly, putting a tentative hand on his arm. The expensive material of his suit was soft beneath her fingers, but his arm was hard and muscular. She had the strangest urge to move closer to him suddenly, and there was nothing sisterly in the thought. He looked down at her, his eyes narrowed, and for a moment she was aware that he was seeing her as something more than a creature who had caused him nothing but inconvenience since her arrival.

'Maria,' he said, rather huskily, and then they were both interrupted as footsteps sounded above and a few seconds later Loren appeared in the curve of the stairs.

Adam moved swiftly away from Maria, almost with relief, Maria thought, and went to meet the other woman. Loren's gaze was speculative as it rested on Maria's flushed cheeks and on the rather attractive picture she made in the cream trousers and scarlet shirt, her chestnut hair swinging naturally to her shoulders. Loren herself, in a clinging gown of deep green crêpe, her hair in its usual coronet, looked quite exquisite, and Maria wondered how anyone could notice anyone else while she was around. The pain she had felt in her head as she fell and which had momentarily dispersed under Adam's influence was returning again, and giving her quite a headache, and with sudden decision she said:

'I – I don't feel very well. Would – would Alice show me where I'm to sleep, and then I'd like to go to bed.'

Adam swung round, leaving Loren. 'What's wrong?' he asked sharply. 'Is it your head?'

Maria flushed. 'Slightly. I – I just feel a bit sick, that's all. Surely you don't mind—'

'Of course we don't mind, Maria.' That was Loren, and she sounded very satisfied with the arrangements.

'I do,' asserted Adam harshly. 'Maria, if you're ill, I'll examine you.'

Maria stared at him tremulously. 'I'm not ill exactly—'

'Then you'll stay and have some dinner,' he commanded briefly, ignoring Loren's horrified amazement.

'Oh, all right, then.' Maria pushed her hands into her pockets. 'But I would like a wash before we eat. Where – where am I to sleep?'

Loren heaved a sigh. 'You're to share the small room with Alice. I'm sorry, Maria, but there are only three bedrooms here, and I couldn't possibly ask you to share my room.'

Adam regarded Maria broodingly. 'Maria can have my room,' he said calmly.

Loren looked at him frowningly. 'But, Adam—'

'This couch will suit me fine,' he replied shortly. 'Now, shall I show Maria where she has to sleep, or will you?'

Loren looked absolutely furious, but there was nothing she could do, and she unwillingly led the way upstairs. Maria went to collect her case, but Adam forestalled her and followed them up, taking the case into the second bedroom where Loren was indicating that Maria could sleep. After they had gone, Maria sank down rather weakly on to the bed. She felt shaken, and it wasn't just the knock she had received on her head. It was something else – something to do with Adam, and she didn't want to think about it.

She showered in the bathroom and changed into a short-skirted dress of mimosa yellow. Combing her hair with deliberately slow movements, she knew she was delaying the moment when she must rejoin her stepbrother and his fiancée, and when she finally descended the stairs she made enough noise to warn them of her arrival. She had no desire to find them in each other's arms.

But when she reached the lounge she thought at first that they had gone out, for there was no sign of them. Then she looked round and saw the french doors at the back of the house were open on to a terrace, and it was here she found them, sitting in the semi-darkness drinking cocktails.

Adam rose when she appeared in the doorway and said: 'Can I get you a drink, Maria? Some fruit juice, or perhaps some sherry.'

Maria squeezed one hand inside the other behind her back. 'I'd prefer a cocktail,' she said clearly. 'I'm not a child, you know, Adam.'

Adam gave a slight bow of his head and she stepped aside to allow him to enter the lounge to get her drink. Then Loren glanced round and said: 'Come out here, Maria. I shan't eat you.'

Maria coloured and was glad of the darkness that hid her embarrassment. She walked out on to the terrace, shivering in the cool breeze. Loren patted the lounger beside her and Maria was forced to go and sit down.

'Well,' said Loren challengingly, 'you certainly have

more spunk than I gave you credit for. Or should I say – more gall?'

Maria stared at her. 'What do you mean?'

Loren gave an exaggerated sigh. 'Oh, darling, don't play games with me. We both know what I'm talking about. I don't think there's any need for us to pretend with each other.'

Maria shook her head. 'Do you mean *my* coming down here?'

'What else?' Loren blew smoke rings expertly into the air.

'Adam insisted that I came.'

'That's what I mean. You've certainly acquired the knack of making him feel a heel.'

'I don't know what you mean.'

'Of course you do, Maria. Oh, I know when you first arrived here, he was pretty annoyed about it, but gradually you've wormed your way into his conscience so that he feels absolutely obliged to put up with you!' Maria gasped and Loren went on: 'You don't imagine Alice usually accompanies us down here, do you?'

Maria got half to her feet, needing to escape from this woman's spiteful tongue, when Adam himself emerged from the house and handed her a glass containing a small quantity of liquid. Maria was forced to take it, and sank back weakly into her seat.

Loren looked up at Adam tantalizingly, and said: 'Has Alice finished the preparations for dinner?'

Adam nodded. 'There was nothing much to do. Mrs. Jennings attended to it all.'

'As usual,' murmured Loren, in a rather self-satisfied way, and cast a mocking glance in Maria's direction.

The evening was a disaster as far as Maria was concerned. She had the greatest difficulty in eating anything, although she managed to swallow something so as not to arouse Adam's curiosity. Even so, she was aware that his gaze rested on her several times during that meal and her colour came and went alarmingly.

At last it was over, and to her relief Loren suggested that she and Adam might go for a drive. Adam looked across at Maria expectantly, and said: 'How does that appeal to you, Maria?'

Maria shook her head a trifle jerkily. 'No, thank you,' she replied shortly. 'I – I'd prefer to go to bed.'

She thought his expression hardened at the abruptness of her response, but she had no heart to be tactful.

'You're all right, aren't you?' he asked sharply. 'I noticed you ate very little at dinner.'

Maria shrugged. 'I'm fine. Just tired, that's all.'

And Adam was forced to accept this. Loren was beginning to look impatient again, and Maria couldn't wait to gain the sanctuary of her room. She had never in all her young life encountered anyone like Loren Griffiths, and she had been right to feel uneasy with her right from the start.

Despite the discomfort of her thoughts, Maria slept almost immediately and awoke next morning to the sound of seagulls crying as they swept low over the cottage. She lay for a moment just listening to their plaintive calls and then slid out of bed and went to the window.

It was still very early, but the shore and the creaming waves beckoned irresistibly, and with determination she shed her pyjamas and put on the one-piece bathing suit she had brought with her. Then she put the cream trousers and her shirt over her bathing suit and fastened her hair in the ponytail with an elastic band. Collecting a towel, she let herself quietly out of her bedroom and went down the stairs. Obviously, no one would be about yet and she had no desire to arouse anybody.

But as she descended the last few stairs a sound made her look round in surprise and she found Adam coming through from the kitchen wearing only navy blue shorts, a towel about his neck. 'Maria!' he exclaimed, in astonishment. 'I thought it must be Alice. It's only six-thirty, you know.'

Maria swallowed hard. 'I – I thought I might go for a swim,' she said. She looked round nervously, half expecting to find Loren Griffiths behind her, but the lounge was deserted. On the couch there were pillows and rugs, and she realized from the tumbled state of their upheaval that Adam must have slept there as he had said he would. He saw her gaze linger on the couch, and said: 'That's right. Loren's still asleep. She won't be up for hours.'

Maria tried to control her embarrassment, and edged towards the door. 'It is all right if I go swimming, isn't it?' she asked, ignoring his observation.

'Of course. I was about to do so myself. Shall we go together?'

Maria lifted her shoulders awkwardly. 'If you like.'

'Good.'

Adam opened the door and they stepped out into the crisp morning air. It was already quite warm, and a faint mist was dispersing on the horizon.

'It looks like being a hot day,' remarked Adam, striding along beside her towards the cliff steps. 'Maybe you'll enjoy it, after all.'

Maria ignored the mocking tone in his voice, and allowed him to descend the steps first so that he could offer her a supporting hand. It was quite a steep flight of steps and she was glad of his company. She would not care to fall from here.

The beach was warm beneath their bare feet, and Maria glanced rather self-consciously at Adam as she began to unbutton her blouse. Adam realized her dilemma, however, and walked ahead, leaving her to take off her outer clothing. To her surprise, he shed his own shorts to reveal a pair of black bathing trunks, and then ran ahead of her into the water, diving cleanly beneath the waves.

Maria hesitated on the brink. The rivulets that rippled round her toes felt freezing and she was loath to plunge her warm body into such iciness. However, she knew it was no use hesitating too long or she really would feel cold, and taking a deep breath she followed Adam's example.

After the initial gasp of chilliness she found it wonderfully exhilarating, and after swimming out some distance, she looked around for Adam. At first she couldn't see him, and then she saw him climbing out on to some rocks, some distance from the shore. He stretched out and waved to her, and with determination she swam towards him. It wasn't far, but by the time she reached him, she was panting, and had hardly the strength to scramble out beside him.

'You should take more exercise,' he remarked lazily. 'Don't you swim at home?'

'Sometimes, but not often,' she admitted. 'Besides, there's no one to swim with. Father never has time, and your mother doesn't swim, does she?'

107

'No,' agreed Adam, rolling on to his stomach and looking down into her face as she lay on her back exposing her body to the warmth of the sun. 'But what about this young man you told me about – Matthew Hurley? Don't you swim with him?'

'No.' Maria wrinkled her nose. Adam's face was disturbingly close to hers, and while he might not be aware of her, she was most certainly aware of him, and his nearness brought back with clarity remembrance of what Loren Griffiths had told her the night before. Was it possible he was only taking some notice of her now to salve his conscience? Was he taking this opportunity before Loren was up because he felt obliged to do so?

She sat up abruptly, and smoothing back her wet hair, looked down into the water. She didn't want that kind of relationship with him. She would rather he ignored her altogether than felt pity for her. She looked across the expanse of water to the shoreline and the cliffs beyond. It was so beautiful here and for a short period she had been enjoying herself, but now Loren's words had destroyed it all and she couldn't stand being so close to him suddenly.

With unselfconsciously graceful movements she slid down into the water, allowing it to close over her head, and struck out strongly for the beach. Once there, she walked to her towel and began to dry herself briskly, not giving herself time to think. She was wringing the excess water out of her hair when Adam came strolling up the beach towards her, looking thoughtful.

'That was sudden, wasn't it?' he remarked, nodding pointedly back towards the rocks. 'One minute you were there, and the next you were gone. What did I say?'

Maria shrugged with assumed nonchalance. 'Nothing,' she denied. 'I just felt like swimming back, that's all.'

Adam studied her sceptically. 'I find that hard to believe, Maria,' he commented dryly.

Maria made an indifferent gesture. 'I don't see why.' She finished towelling her hair and began to pull on the cream slacks.

'Now, hold it!' Adam put a detaining hand on her arm, preventing her from stepping into the trousers. 'You're wet and you'll ruin your clothes. Sit down for a while and let the sun take the wetness out of your swimsuit.'

Maria looked up at him defiantly. 'You don't have to put yourself out for me, you know. I can look after myself.'

'What are you talking about now?' Adam stared at her.

Maria shrugged again. 'Well, I just don't need you to – to keep me company. I'm quite used to being on my own.'

'In heaven's name, what's got into you?' Adam grasped her wrist. 'A few moments ago you seemed quite glad of my company, and now you're behaving as though I tried to assault you or something.'

Maria bit her lip hard. 'If that's the impression you've received, then you couldn't be more wrong!' she exclaimed, trying to unfasten his fingers from her wrist with her free hand.

'Then what is wrong?' asked Adam harshly, resisting all her efforts to release herself. His eyes narrowed. 'Has Loren said something to you?'

Maria wouldn't look at him, and he lifted her chin and stared down at her mutinous face searchingly. 'So she has said something,' he said resignedly. 'I should have known.'

Maria had no desire to cause any more trouble with Loren, and she shook her head out of his grasp vigorously. 'What could she have said?' she retaliated. 'It's nothing like that. I just don't want you to feel you have to entertain me.'

Adam gave an exasperated sigh. 'I don't *feel* I have to entertain you. This may come as a surprise, but I was quite enjoying your company until now.' He let her go. 'But if you want to go back . . .'

Maria watched him bend and lift his towel and begin rubbing his chest. For a moment he stared out to sea, his expression brooding, and she was able to observe him undetected. He was certainly an attractive man, and she could understand Loren's fascination with him. There wasn't an ounce of superfluous flesh on his hard body. His hair lay thick and smooth against his head, and yet there was a sensitivity in the length of his fingers and in the penetrating darkness of his eyes. She realized so many things that had not been evident to her from the schoolgirlish impressions of five years ago and she wondered for the first time whether her reasons for coming to London had been wholly concerned with escaping from the confinement of life in Kilcarney or whether deep inside her she had been unconsciously longing to see Adam again.

He turned suddenly and caught her eyes upon him and for a moment he looked at her, holding her gaze until, colouring, she looked away.

'Don't go,' he said. 'Not yet.'

Maria's legs felt weak even while she despised herself for being so submissive. 'All right,' she said, and spreading her towel she sat down on it.

He did the same, subsiding beside her, stretching his arms above his head, flattening his stomach muscles. Then he turned his head to one side and looked at her quizzically. 'Do you realize that's almost the first time you've done something I asked you without causing an argument?'

Maria rested her arms along her legs, leaning forward, allowing her loosened hair to fall like a wet curtain against her cheeks. The sun was hotter now, and she could feel it warm against her cool skin. She would have liked nothing better than to spend the whole day on the beach, but soon they would have to go back and the prospect was depressing.

'Have you decided what course you intend taking?' Adam asked suddenly, propping himself up on his elbows. 'Janet told me she had phoned you.'

Maria glanced round at him. 'I wanted to discuss it with you,' she said. 'I suppose you would say I should take the course that is already in progress.'

Adam's eyes narrowed. 'I could say that you chose a rather inconvenient time to arrive to take any course,' he returned sardonically. 'However, in my opinion you would be better advised to wait until after the summer break.'

Maria's eyes widened. 'But that's over three months away.'

'I know.'

'And what am I expected to do during the time between now and then? Go home?'

Adam shrugged and lay back. 'That's up to you.'

'You mean, you'd let me stay?' She was incredulous.

'Could I stop you?'

'You know you could.' Maria stared at him exasperatedly. 'Don't tease me, Adam, please. What should I do?'

He regarded her steadily. 'You must decide for yourself. You're the one who gets bored within four walls, remember.'

Maria pressed her lips together and returned to her contemplation of the horizon. She was disconcerted by the change in his attitude, and she wasn't at all sure any more what she should do.

'I – I'll think about it,' she said quietly.

'You do that.' Adam closed his eyes, and thereafter there was silence for a long while. Maria thought he had gone to sleep and relaxed herself. It was very pleasant just sitting there allowing the sun to dry her swimsuit and her hair. She found Adam more disturbing in this conciliatory mood than when he was angry with her, and she wondered whether this change of tactics on his part was deliberate. Maybe he had realized he was getting nowhere being belligerent.

Time passed all too quickly, however, and eventually Adam roused himself and sat up, glancing at his wristwatch. 'Time we were getting back for breakfast,' he remarked lazily. 'Alice will be up and about by now and I don't know about you, but I'm hungry.'

Maria got obediently to her feet, shaking the sand out of her towel, and pulled on her shirt and trousers. 'It must be quite a change for Alice, coming down here,' she murmured insinuatingly, unable to resist the remark.

Adam glanced across at her quickly, and then frowned. 'No more than for any of us,' he replied sharply. 'Do I denote an innuendo somewhere?'

Maria shrugged, coloured, and wished she had kept her mouth shut. This past hour in Adam's company had been wholly delightful, and now she had spoiled it by her own spitefulness.

Slinging her towel over her shoulder, she turned away and began to walk towards the steps, but he caught the back of her neck and halted her progress. He was close behind her and she could feel the heat of his body. 'Maria!' he said insistently. 'You didn't answer me.'

Maria refused to face him. 'You're too sensitive, Adam,' she said huskily. 'I didn't mean anything.'

'Oh, yes, you did. If I've learned nothing else about you, I do know when you're being provocative. Are you implying that Alice's presence here is a novelty?' His grip tightened. 'Are you?'

'You're hurting me!' Maria tried to push his hand away.

'You deserve to be hurt,' he muttered, giving her a shake.

Maria lost her balance and fell back against him, and for a moment her body was against his. It was only a moment, but Adam thrust her away without saying another word and turning walked back to where he had left his towel. Trembling, Maria stumbled across to the cliff steps, mounting them on unsteady legs. It had only been a moment, and most likely his anger had got the better of him, but just for a moment she had sensed an awareness in him, and she had known with feminine instinct that as his fingers slid across her shoulders they had wanted to linger . . .

CHAPTER SEVEN

THE Bellamy College of Technology was a twenty-minute bus journey from the bus stop at the end of Virginia Grove. Maria discovered this on Tuesday morning as she attended her interview with the principal. When she had telephoned him on Monday afternoon and explained the position to him, he had suggested that she might like to come along and discuss it with him, and she had been only too glad to agree. But then, yesterday, she had been still raw from her experiences at the week-end.

From the moment she arrived back at the villa with Adam after their swim on Sunday morning she had longed to get away, and Loren's malicious reactions to everything she did became unbearable. She had been immensely relieved when Loren took Adam off on Sunday afternoon to visit some friends and they did not arrive back until after she had gone to bed.

On Monday morning she had deliberately stayed in bed until after she heard Alice about, and when Adam came back with damp hair from the beach she avoided his questioning gaze.

They arrived back in London soon after eleven, and Adam dropped Maria off first, saying he was driving to the hospital to visit a patient after he had seen Loren home. Thereafter, she did not see him for the rest of the day, and was forced to put on a show of having enjoyed herself for Mrs. Lacey's benefit.

Her interview with the principal of the college was a success, and when she tentatively suggested that she might join the current class he agreed, saying he was certain she would not find it difficult to catch up with what had gone before. She emerged from the building feeling a surge of confidence, and a lightening of spirits when she realized that as from tomorrow she would be fully occupied instead of just loafing about.

She walked back to Virginia Grove and told Mrs. Lacey, and the housekeeper nodded her encouragement. 'It will be nice for you, meeting people of your own age,' she commented. 'This house is too dull for someone like you.'

Maria was about to contradict her and then stopped herself. It was as well if Mrs. Lacey did think she found the house, and its occupants, dull. That way she would not be expected to spend too much time in it.

The telephone pealed and Mrs. Lacey sighed. 'I'll answer it,' said Maria quickly, and went to lift the receiver. To her surprise it was David Hallam.

'Hi!' he said. 'Remember me?'

'Of course,' Maria smiled. 'What do you want?'

'You,' he answered, laughingly. 'I said I'd ring. Did you think I wouldn't?'

'I never thought about it,' replied Maria honestly.

David snorted. 'Well, that's straight enough,' he said dryly. 'But seriously, what are you doing today?'

'Right now? Helping Mrs. Lacey prepare lunch.'

'How do you fancy coming over to our place this afternoon? I'm giving a party, and I thought you might like to come along. I'd pick you up, of course.'

Maria hesitated. 'All right,' she said slowly. 'What time?'

After she had arranged a time with David, he rang off, and she went to find Mrs. Lacey and tell her.

'Does Mr. Adam know, miss?'

'How could he? I didn't know myself until a few minutes ago. I'll tell him at lunch time. I have to tell him about the commercial course as well.'

'I'm sorry, miss, Mr. Adam won't be in to lunch. He rang just a few minutes before you got back to say that Mrs. Ainsley has had a relapse and they're having to operate again this afternoon. It's touch and go, he said.'

'Oh!' Maria bit her lip. 'That's the old lady who fell downstairs, isn't it?'

'That's right, miss.'

Maria shook her head. 'Oh, what a shame!'

Mrs. Lacey shrugged. 'She's old,' she said, with a sigh. 'Age is her worst enemy.'

Maria turned away. Somehow it seemed dreadful contemplating attending a party at David's when people were critically ill – dying, even. It was an inconsequential thought. People were dying all the time. Even so, it made her realize how lucky she really was, and mocked the self-pity she had experienced yesterday and the day before when Loren was being bitchy to her.

The party at David's was a huge success. Maria was relieved to find that Larry Hadley was not there, but Evelyn James was, and she viewed Maria with calculating eyes when she saw how attentive David was being.

David's home was a large old house set in its own grounds, and his parents had installed tennis courts and a swimming pool. There were about thirty young people lounging about the pool, or running energetically about on the courts, and Maria was glad she had brought her swimsuit.

After introducing her to his mother, David constituted himself her guide and companion. Although he introduced her to many of his other guests, some of whom she recognized from the visit she had paid to the tennis club with Larry, he made it plain that for the afternoon she was with him.

She changed into her swimsuit in one of the cabins provided and then they sat by the pool, drinking Cokes and talking. It was another hot afternoon and Maria wondered how all these young people could afford to spend the whole afternoon doing nothing. Surely some of them had jobs of work to do.

'You were away over the week-end,' remarked David, lounging on an air-bed beside her. 'I rang twice.'

Maria smiled, smoothing her hair behind her ears. 'Did you? Yes, I went down to Kent with Adam and Loren Griffiths.'

David smiled. 'Ah, yes, the fair Loren,' he observed lightly. 'What did you think of her?'

Maria shrugged. 'I hardly know her.'

'That's a tactful answer,' David chuckled. 'Did she start digging in her claws?'

'I don't know what you mean.'

'Sure you do. You'll have gathered by now that she considers your stepbrother her man.'

Maria sighed impatiently. 'So everyone says!'

David watched her with amused eyes. 'But you don't think so?' He smiled lazily. 'Nor do I. I think your stepbrother is nobody's man. He's not the type to let a woman walk all over him.'

'Don't you think so?'

David shook his head. 'No. And that's what fascinates Loren Griffiths.'

'You seem very knowledgeable about him.'

'I've known him a long time. My parents knew the family before Adam's father died.'

'Oh, I see,' Maria nodded.

'And Adam's mother married your father – that's right, isn't it?' Maria nodded and David went on: 'But what brought you to England? Did Adam invite you?'

Maria shook her head. 'No. I'm going to take a commercial course. I start at the Bellamy College tomorrow.'

'Tomorrow? So soon?'

'Well, I'm joining a class that has already been working for several weeks. I have to make up for lost time. Otherwise I shall have to wait until September to begin.'

David frowned. 'Then wait until September. Hell, the weather is just beginning to improve. We could have some great times together.'

'Don't you have a job either?'

David sighed and stretched out lazily. 'Not until September. Then I'm joining the business. My father's business.'

'Oh, yes, he's a solicitor, isn't he?'

'Did Larry tell you?'

'Yes.' Maria glanced round. 'He's not here, is he?'

David shook his head. 'No, I thought it better not to invite him in the circumstances.'

'What circumstances?' Maria stared at him.

'You being here.' David narrowed his eyes to look at her.

Maria sighed. 'But why should that matter? We're only friends, after all.'

David caught her fingers in his. 'Who?' he questioned softly. 'You and Larry – or you and me?'

Maria flushed. 'All of us.'

David propped himself up to regard her searchingly. 'I think we could be more than just friends,' he murmured huskily. He slid his fingers along her arm, and with a gentle but firm gesture, she disentangled herself. David was a nice boy, she liked him, more than she liked Larry actually, but that was all. She had no intention of getting involved with anybody, and after a moment David gave an expressive shrug of his shoulders and lay back again.

Although David's mother invited her to stay for dinner and meet his father, Maria refused. She had been away from the house almost the whole day one way and another and she knew she wanted to see Adam – to talk to him.

But after bidding David good-bye she entered the house to find he was not yet home.

Mrs. Lacey gave a resigned sigh. 'I expect he's still at the hospital,' she said. 'He'll likely go straight to surgery, so you might as well have your meal.'

Maria hesitated, and then nodded her assent. She might as well eat now. There was no real guarantee that Adam would come straight home after surgery.

It was in fact almost eleven o'clock when Adam arrived home. Mrs. Lacey had gone to bed and even Maria was on the point of going up. She felt depressed and angry at having to wait so long to speak to him, and she thought how thoughtless he was going straight to Loren Griffiths without even bothering to telephone after surgery. It crossed her mind that he might have had no evening meal, but that didn't prevent her feeling alone and rejected.

She remained curled up on the couch in the lounge and she heard him cross the hall and push open the lounge door without turning her head. He had seen the light of the lamps, of course, but she would not make any effort to acknowledge his presence.

He came into the room, unfastening the jacket of his dark suit, and taking out his case of cigars. He glanced in her direction, but she concentrated hard on the book in her lap, and didn't look up.

'I thought you'd be in bed,' he said abruptly, lighting a cigar.

Maria looked up then. 'Did you? Well, as you can see, I'm not.'

Adam inhaled deeply. 'Is there any coffee available? Did Mrs. Lacey leave any for me?'

Maria assumed an indifferent expression. 'You'd better look in the kitchen,' she said. 'I haven't the faintest idea.'

Adam regarded her for a moment longer and then strode out of the room. After he had gone, Maria felt ashamed. She could have gone and got him some coffee. It wasn't much to ask, not when he was offering her his hospitality.

She slid off the couch and walked through to the hall. There was a light showing under the kitchen door and with a determined effort she opened the door and went in. Adam was filling the percolator as she entered and after giving her a cursory glance he concentrated on what he was doing.

Maria bit her lip. 'Didn't Mrs. Lacey leave you anything?'

'Obviously not.' Adam spread his hand eloquently. 'What do you want? I thought you were engrossed in your book.'

Maria sighed. 'You're very late,' she said, trying not to feel indignant. After all, he was the one who was late. She ought not to be feeling guilty at not running after him when he had chosen to stay out until this hour.

'Yes.' Adam sounded bored.

Maria hesitated. 'I – I wanted to talk to you.'

'Oh, yes. What about? Couldn't it wait until morning?'

'No. That is – well, I'm starting at the commercial college tomorrow.'

Adam looked up from examining the contents of the fridge. 'Tomorrow?' he echoed uncomprehendingly. 'I know nothing about it!'

'No. That's why I stayed up. To tell you. I saw the principal this morning.'

Adam straightened. 'You're joining this course that has already begun?'

'Yes.'

'Do you think that's wise? After all, it's all new to you.'

Maria twisted her hands together. 'I can hardly hang about here for three months, doing nothing.'

Adam shrugged. 'Oh, well, it's your decision.'

Maria heaved an exasperated sigh. 'Heavens, you're behaving as though you didn't want me to take the course, after all! I thought you'd be glad to get me out of your hair.'

Adam's expression hardened. 'I don't recall passing any opinion on the subject,' he replied harshly. 'No doubt you'll do as you choose, as usual.'

Maria stared at him impatiently. 'I have deliberately waited up to discuss it with you!' she exclaimed angrily. 'I can't help it if you don't come home much before midnight and I have to spring it on you when you're tired and obviously ill-tempered!'

Adam came across to her, his eyes burning with suppressed violence. 'One day, Maria, you'll go too far!' he said fiercely. 'I don't have to take that kind of talk from anyone, least of all you!'

Maria grimaced and turned away. 'I'm going to bed!' she said unsteadily. 'It's obvious you're in a foul mood. I'm sorry you didn't get a prodigal's welcome, but quite honestly I thought Miss Griffiths would have looked after you more than adequately—'

Adam's fingers closed on her shoulders and he swung her round to face him, his eyes blazing. 'It may interest you to know that I have not seen Miss Griffiths this evening,' he muttered savagely. 'I've just come from St. Michael's Hospital. Mrs. Ainsley died half an hour ago.'

'Oh!' Maria pressed a horrified hand to her mouth. 'Oh, Adam! I'm – I'm sorry!'

Adam released her abruptly, and turned away, a muscle jerking in his cheek. 'Go to bed!' he said heavily. 'As you pointed out, I'm not the best of company.'

Maria chewed unhappily at her lower lip. 'Go and sit down, Adam,' she said, 'I'll make the coffee.'

'That won't be necessary.' Adam's voice was cold. He took a beaker from the wall cupboard and glanced at the percolator that was beginning to bubble.

'Oh, please, let me do it.' Maria moved miserably. 'You must be hungry, too. Have you had anything to eat?'

Adam turned and looked at her. 'No, but I'm not hungry. And I don't need your assistance either. Just go and leave me alone.'

Maria hesitated only a moment longer and then without a word she left the kitchen. It was her own fault, she had only herself to blame, she was too eager to jump to conclusions where Adam was concerned. She was far too sensitive, and after all, it was nothing to her if he spent every evening with his fiancée. Or at least, it shouldn't be . . .

Maria didn't see Adam at breakfast next morning. He had had an early call and consequently she had left for the college before he got back. It wasn't until she was on the bus going to the college that she realized she had forgotten to mention that she had been to David's home the day before. But then their conversation the previous evening had been stilted, to say the least, and she doubted whether he would be interested in anything she did after this.

Her first day passed off reasonably quickly. Her vague imaginings of what the course might entail were swiftly dispelled when it was revealed that as well as taking shorthand, typewriting and English, she was also expected to learn commerce and accounting. She was given a list of textbooks she would need, and straight after taking lunch in the college canteen she went to buy them. She arrived back at Adam's house about four-thirty in the afternoon, her arms full of books and paper, and a comprehensive amount of homework to do.

Adam was in the lounge when she came in, and viewed her loaded arms with narrowed eyes. 'You don't propose to work all evening as well as all day, do you?' he queried shortly.

Maria dumped the load on to an armchair and shook her aching arms. 'Why not?'

Adam got to his feet, and came across to lift one of the textbooks indifferently. Maria stood linking her fingers together, watching him, and presently he looked at her nervous face. 'It's not necessary, you know,' he remarked rather disparagingly.

'What's not necessary?' Maria didn't understand him.

Adam threw the textbook down. 'All this!' He flexed his muscles. 'I'm quite prepared to accept that you found life in Kilcarney confining and you felt like escaping for a while. You don't have to take this course if you don't want to. I shan't object if you stay on for a while.'

Maria stared at him indignantly. 'You think I came here with no intention of actually taking a course, is that it?'

Adam shrugged. 'Oh, no. I think your intentions were clear enough. It's just not necessary, that's all.'

Maria heaved a sigh. 'But you got your receptionist to find out about these things for me.'

'Knowing that there would be no course starting before the summer break,' retorted Adam impatiently. 'I assumed you would wait until then before committing yourself.'

'And committing you!' exclaimed Maria angrily. 'So long as I'm freelance, you can pack me off whenever you feel like it!'

Adam's expression darkened. 'I hope you know what you're doing, then. These courses can take as long as a year.'

'This is a private course. It doesn't take as long!'

'I daresay you've forgotten there'll be the summer break, anyway.'

Maria compressed her lips. She had forgotten. That would be two months wasted.

'I – I shall go home for the summer break,' she replied decisively. 'Now – if you'll excuse me . . .'

Adam caught her arm. 'Don't work this evening.'

'Why not?' Maria tossed her head.

'Because it's too much. You've only just begun. Give yourself time to adapt or you'll make yourself ill. Besides, it's much too warm.'

Maria tucked her hair behind her ear with her loose hand. 'I've nothing better to do!' she retorted.

'Yes, you have.' Adam's thumb moved against her flesh. 'I've got to go and see a private patient of mine at Staines. You could come with me.'

A quiver ran up Maria's spine, and the hot colour flooded her cheeks. She would like nothing better than to spend the evening with Adam, but something warned her that she should not. It wasn't that she was afraid of him; she knew he was trustworthy, it was herself she was worried about. She was half scared there might come a moment when he became aware of her as he had last week-end on the beach, and she might succumb to the temptation to make that aware-ness physical as well as mental. He might think she was still a child, but she knew she was not, and the feelings she experienced towards Adam must not be stimu-lated.

'Th – thank you, but no,' she murmured now. 'I – I must get on. I promised my tutor, Mr. Lawson, that I would try and have some of this learned by tomorrow.'

Adam released her. 'Very well,' he said, his voice cool again. 'Forget it!'

During the following week Maria saw little of Adam. He seemed constantly on call, and even their mealtimes together had to be curtailed. He rarely asked about her work, and as she found it difficult to relax with him, they spoke little. Once or twice she tried to bring up the subject of David Hallam, but it wasn't easy when her tentative overtures met with such a degree of coolness.

She knew he wasn't seeing a lot of Loren Griffiths either. The actress rang several times, and Maria was glad when Mrs. Lacey took the calls. Larry Hadley rang, too, but Maria refused all invitations, giving herself plenty of time to cope with her homework.

Over the week-end, she did accept an invitation to tennis on Sunday afternoon at David's, and this time she met his father. Victor Hallam was like his son, both in looks and personality, and Maria found herself talking to him quite naturally, discussing her ideas about making use of one's time, taking sides with him against David's assumed indolence.

She wasn't sure how Adam spent the week-end. She knew he was on call, of course, and was glad he was not at home when she arrived back from the Hallams'.

The following Thursday morning he came down to breakfast looking dark-browed and truculent. He took his seat opposite her without issuing his usual brief greeting, and she looked across at him apprehensively. What now?

Passing him his coffee, she avoided his eyes, and he said harshly: 'Why didn't you tell me you've been going out with David Hallam?'

Maria coloured. 'I – er – I didn't think you'd be interested,' she murmured awkwardly.

Adam clenched his fist. 'You didn't think I'd be interested,' he repeated bleakly. 'Why not?'

Maria swallowed hard. 'Well, I've only been out with him twice,' she volunteered uncomfortably.

126

'You've been to his home twice, which is a vastly different thing!' snapped Adam angrily. 'Surely he told you the Hallams were friends of mine.'

'Well – well, yes.'

'And didn't it occur to you that I'd look pretty damn silly if they mentioned you two were friends and I knew nothing about it?' He sounded furious.

Maria bent her head. 'I – I was going to tell you. I – I haven't had much chance!'

'In ten days? You must be joking!'

'Oh, Adam, it's not important.'

'Damn you, isn't it? I don't like being made a fool of!' He rose abruptly to his feet. 'I understood you were to spend your time catching up on your fellow students, not lounging around the Hallams' pool!'

Maria looked up at him indignantly. 'I can't work all the time. You said so yourself.'

'And yet you refused to come down to Staines with me.' Adam stared at her coldly.

Maria's eyes widened. 'What's the matter?' she taunted him angrily. 'Are you jealous?'

As soon as the words were out, she wanted to retract them. It was such a ridiculous thing to say. Adam – jealous of her!

Adam regarded her contemptuously for a moment, and then he strode out into the hall, just as Mrs. Lacey was coming in carrying his ham and eggs. She stared at him in consternation.

'What's wrong?' she asked. 'I didn't hear the phone.'

'There's nothing wrong, Mrs. Lacey,' returned Adam curtly. 'I don't want anything else, thank you.'

And with that he slammed out of the house.

Maria sat motionless, controlling the trembling sensation that threatened to sweep over her body. Mrs. Lacey carried the tray to the table and put it down uncomprehendingly. She looked at Maria's frozen features, and clicked her tongue.

'Now what's the matter?' she exclaimed impatiently. 'I've never known Mr. Adam do that before.'

Maria shivered violently. 'Do what?' she asked, pretending not to understand.

'Go without his breakfast,' retorted Mrs. Lacey heavily. 'Whatever have you been saying to him, miss?'

Maria got up from her seat. 'We just had a – a difference of opinion, that's all,' she replied. 'I – er – I don't want anything either.'

'And what am I do to with all this?' cried Mrs. Lacey indicating the laden tray of ham, eggs and toast.

Maria shook her head. 'Eat it yourself?' she suggested, with an attempt at lightness, and went out to collect her books for college.

The whole day seemed blighted. Mr. Lawson wasn't in the best of tempers to begin with, and as the weather was close and thundery, it didn't help matters. Maria was all thumbs, hitting the wrong keys on the typewriter until Mr. Lawson grew impatient with her carelessness, and reduced her almost to tears.

It was a relief when four o'clock came and she could escape. Gathering up her books, she left by the main entrance, running down the steps to the street. A car like Adam's was parked near the entrance, but she didn't pay it much attention until the door was thrust open and Adam said: 'Get in!' in tones that brooked no argument.

Maria obeyed, sliding into the front beside him rather nervously. 'This is a – surprise,' she murmured awkwardly.

'I thought it looked like rain,' returned Adam, putting the car into gear.

Maria looked up. The sky was very overcast, and a faint rumble of thunder could be heard in the distance.

'Thank you,' was all she could think of to say, and with a brief nod he set the car in motion.

Adam didn't drive to Kensington, however. He turned in the opposite direction, crossing the Thames and continuing on the road towards Richmond. Maria glanced at him anxiously. To begin with, she had thought he intended calling at the hospital, but when he by-passed that she didn't know where he was taking her.

As though sensing her discomfort, he cast a look in her direction. 'I thought we might have afternoon tea at a place I know near the river,' he remarked quietly. 'If you have no objections.'

'Of course not.' Maria compressed her lips.

'Good.' Adam returned to concentrating on his driving and for a while the only sound was that of the engine.

Eventually he turned between the gates of a roadhouse that was set back from the road and whose rear approaches were those of the river. The thunder seemed to have receded somewhat, although the air was still heavy when Adam parked the Rover in the car park. Maria slid out without waiting for his assistance, and after he had locked the car's doors they walked up to the entrance.

A verandah ran right round the building, and following Adam Maria noticed that at the back of the building there was a small landing stage with one or two boats tied up to it. Willows drooped right down to the water's edge, providing shade on sunny afternoons. It was very attractive, and Maria forgot her apprehension in appreciating her surroundings.

However, there were few people about, and the proprietor came across to Adam with a wide smile. 'Hi there,' he said, leaving Maria in no doubt that they were old acquaintances. 'What can I offer you today?'

Adam grinned, raking a hand through his hair and looking considerably younger than when his face was sombre. 'Just afternoon tea, Bert, and some of Linda's home-made scones.'

'All right,' Bert nodded, and went away to get their order while Adam indicated that they should sit at the table on the verandah, by the rail, overlooking the landing stage and the river beyond.

Maria took her seat rather nervously and looked at the river where a family of ducklings were diving among the reeds. It was very peaceful here. It was hard to believe they were only a few miles from London. Cupping her chin on one hand, she shook back her hair and breathed a sigh. Then she became aware of Adam's scrutiny, and tried not to notice.

'Mrs. Lacey will wonder where you are,' he commented wryly.

Maria glanced quickly at him. 'Didn't you tell her you intended meeting me?'

'No.' He was abrupt.

'Why?'

He shrugged, lighting a cheroot. 'I'm not in the habit of issuing an account of my movements unless I'm on call, and this afternoon I'm not.'

Maria pressed her lips together. 'She'll worry. I'm usually home by four-thirty.'

Adam raised his eyebrows indifferently, and she looked away, wondering whether she ought to go into the roadhouse and ask to use the telephone. Then it occurred to her, for no apparent reason, that Adam might not want Mrs. Lacey to know he had taken his stepsister for tea. If Loren Griffiths rang, Mrs. Lacey would be sure to tell her, and that would not please the other woman.

Maria bit her lip, and Adam looked at her broodingly. 'For God's sake, go and telephone if it means that much to you,' he snapped. 'Surely Mrs. Lacey won't call out a search party because you're half an hour later than usual?'

Maria could have pointed out that she was going to be much later than a mere half hour, but she kept such thoughts to herself and presently the man Bert returned with a tray containing tea for two, hot scones with jam and cream, and a selection of tiny cakes. He placed the tray in front of Maria, and after he had left them she took charge of it, pouring the tea and offering it to Adam.

Adam drank two cups of tea, but ate nothing, and it was left to Maria to show that the scones were as delicious as they appeared. Even so, she wasn't very hungry herself, and she was relieved when Adam stubbed out his cheroot and asked if she was ready to leave.

He said good-bye to Bert, stopping in the kitchen doorway to have a word with Bert's wife, Linda, and then they walked back to the car. He unlocked Maria's door and she climbed in hastily, smoothing her short skirt over her thighs. He walked round the bonnet and slid in beside her and she thought with a thrill of excitement how different their relationship was now from when she had last seen him all those years ago in Kilcarney. Then she had been a schoolgirl, with little to commend her in a navy gymslip and white shirtblouse. She couldn't recall him saying anything in particular to her, although he had pulled her ponytail a couple of times, and teased her about her adolescent chatter. Maybe he had expected her to be the same. One tended to remember things as they were and never credited the maturity that was bound to follow. With Adam it was different. Five years ago he had looked very much as he looked now, but now she was a woman and no longer a child.

Adam loosened his collar and pulled down his tie. 'It's damn hot!' he muttered, starting the car. He glanced once at Maria, noting the attractive picture she made in a sleeveless red and white candy-striped dress, the short skirt of which cooled her legs, and the sudden colour in her cheeks owed less to the temperature of the weather than to her own disturbed emotions.

Adam swung the Rover out of the parking area and halted at the entrance, looking critically to right and left. 'It's a pity we don't have any swimming gear,' he commented dryly. 'I know a spot not far from here where we could swim.'

Maria nodded. 'That sounds nice,' she murmured awkwardly, and he looked quickly at her.

'You're not suggesting we should disregard the conventions, are you?' he inquired harshly.

Maria's eyes widened. 'Of course not.' Her cheeks burned.

Adam raised his dark eyebrows. 'You surprise me. With your modern outlook on life, I wouldn't have thought you would consider it essential to have swimming gear!' His tone was deliberately scathing.

Maria turned her head away, concentrating on an insect that was trying desperately to escape through a pane of glass. 'You have no right to say that to me!' she said tautly. 'Is that why you brought me here? To humiliate me in whatever way you choose?'

Adam rammed the car into gear, and turned abruptly out on to the road, heading back towards town. He did not speak, and for the life of her Maria could not have carried on any conversation if he had. After the tense few minutes they had just spent, she felt limp and shaken, and she couldn't conceive why Adam should have wanted to be so cruel. For a moment he had looked at her as though he hated her, and it had left her weak and trembling.

They encountered a traffic jam on the outskirts of the city, but Adam turned off the main highways, threading his way through a maze of side streets until they emerged in the road off which Virginia Grove branched.

He stopped the car at the foot of the Grove, and leaning past her thrust open her door. For a moment, the hardness of his body was against hers and she could smell the faint aroma of tobacco, shaving lotion and body heat that emanated from him. And in that moment, she wanted to touch him, too, so much that she had to grip her books very tightly to prevent herself from doing so.

'Th – thank you,' she managed, rather stiffly, and slid out, and without a word Adam slammed the door again and drove away.

CHAPTER EIGHT

For the remainder of the week Maria saw little of Adam, and she told herself she was glad. She was kept busy at the college and during the evenings she was adequately occupied with her studies. Larry Hadley rang on Saturday morning to ask her to go to the tennis club with him, and deciding that this was the best method of showing David that she had no intention of becoming seriously involved with either of them, she accepted. However, David was there, and he and Larry spent the afternoon eyeing one another with only lightly veiled hostility.

On Sunday, Maria sunbathed in the garden in the morning. Adam disappeared after breakfast, and Mrs. Lacey told her he had gone to play golf with one of his colleagues. During the afternoon she read. Adam did not come home for lunch, and it was early evening before she heard his car in the drive. And then she didn't see him. He came home, changed, and disappeared again before dinner. She didn't have to ask where he had gone. She could guess.

Towards the middle of the following week Adam arrived home for dinner one evening and dropped a white envelope in front of Maria. Maria, who had only exchanged distant pleasantries with him for the past week, looked up in surprise.

His eyes regarded her challengingly, and he said: 'It's an invitation. Open it!'

Maria hesitated, and then obediently slit open the envelope. Inside was a white card engraved with gold lettering. To her astonishment she found it was from Loren Griffiths, asking her to a buffet dinner party at her London house on Friday evening.

Maria read the invitation a second time, and then looked blankly up at Adam. 'Why have I been invited?' she asked, more calmly than she felt.

Adam lifted his shoulders indifferently. 'I imagine because she thought you might enjoy it.'

Maria dropped her eyes before he could read the scepticism in them. 'Well – I shan't go, of course.'

'Why?' Adam was abrupt.

Maria sighed. 'Because I shan't know anybody there. Loren Griffiths' friends aren't my friends.'

'I shall be there.'

'Yes – yes, I know.' Maria bit her lip. She could hardly point out that she was unlikely to see much of Adam if Loren was around. 'Besides,' she went on, searching for excuses, 'I've nothing suitable to wear.'

'You have plenty of time to buy something.'

Maria compressed her lips. 'All right, then,' she said reluctantly, 'I just don't want to go.'

Adam uttered an exclamation. 'Why, for heaven's sake? I thought you might find it exciting.'

'*You* thought?' Maria looked up. 'So you suggested I should be invited. I might have known!'

Adam raked his hand through his hair. 'I'm endeavouring to keep my patience, Maria, but you're making it damned difficult!'

Maria put the card back inside its envelope. 'You don't have to bother about me. I've told you before—'

'Blast you, you'll tell me nothing,' he snapped violently. 'Loren has invited you and the least you can do, in all decency, is accept.'

Maria shook her head. 'But she doesn't even like me,' she protested.

'You hardly know her,' retorted Adam. 'Why should you imagine she doesn't like you?'

Maria shrugged, unwilling to enter into arguments with him over her relationship with Loren. 'That's beside the point,' she said.

'Then what is the point?' enquired Adam sarcastically. 'What excuse will you make when you refuse her invitation? Shall I tell her you aren't old enough to attend such an adult function, or would you like to tell her yourself?'

Maria was stung by his derisory tone. 'I just don't want to be involved, that's all,' she exclaimed. 'Why should she suddenly decide to invite me? Does she need to demonstrate yet again that you're her property?'

Adam looked as though he would have liked to use physical violence against her then, and she shrank back from the glare in his dark eyes. 'What a miserable little mind you have, Maria,' he bit out contemptuously. 'You have some ridiculous notion that the relationship between Loren and myself is an unconventional one. You need to categorize everything, put people, like things, into slots – well, it can't be done. And the sooner you realize it, the better.'

'I don't know what you mean.' Maria's cheeks burned.

'Oh yes, you do. You're constantly probing, trying to suggest that so far as Loren is concerned I have no will of my own. It may interest you to know that I enjoy our relationship!'

Maria got to her feet. 'I don't want to know anything about it,' she cried, breathing quickly. 'And you can tell Loren Griffiths anything you like as far as I'm concerned!' And with that she ran from the room.

In her bedroom, she flung herself on the bed, burying her face in the soft coverings. Adam could be so cruel, and she was a fool to allow him to hurt her so. But almost without her becoming aware of it, everything Adam said or did had become important to her and the gnawing anxieties he aroused inside her could no longer be ignored. Her reasons for avoiding Loren Griffiths' party were less to do with the actress herself than with the torture of seeing Adam with her, close to her, talking to her, making love to her . . .

She pressed a trembling hand to her mouth. She must stop thinking like this. No matter what happened, Adam saw her only as a child, as his stepsister, and their involvement with one another was coloured by his mother's relationship to her father. Without that relationship, he would never have noticed her at all. He met dozens of girls like her in the course of his work, girls to be smiled at, spoken to, and then passed over. But when it came to emotional affairs, he chose someone like Loren, a woman as beautiful and sophisticated as she was experienced, and capable of satisfying him in every way. She was immature, as he had said, and her refusal to accept Loren's invitation was proof of that.

Biting her lips, she slid purposefully off the bed. She would prove she was not a child. She would attend Loren's party and show Adam that she could be adult and interesting to other men if not to him.

When she entered the dining-room again, she found Adam scanning the evening paper as he helped himself to some of Mrs. Lacey's delicious strawberry shortcake, and she thought with a rising sense of frustration that their argument had had no visible effects on him.

He looked up as she came to stand by the table, and said: 'Mrs. Lacey took your dinner away. She thought you could not be hungry.'

Maria compressed her lips. 'I'm not,' she replied tightly, and then, gathering her small store of confidence, she went on: 'You can tell Miss Griffiths that I shall be pleased to accept the invitation to her party.'

Adam's eyes narrowed. 'You're going?'

'Yes.'

He lifted his shoulders in an eloquent gesture. 'Very well,' he responded coolly. 'I shall take you myself. Be ready about nine.'

Maria was about to say that she would rather make her own way there, but then she realized that to do so would sound childish too, as indeed it was. 'All right,' she said, nodding. 'Thank you.'

On Friday evening Maria spent hours in her room getting ready. She was determined to look her best and she wished Geraldine was on hand to advise her. In the past, Adam's mother had taken an active interest in helping her to choose her clothes, and without her guidance Maria's father would have considered the kind of clothes she wore unsuitable and extravagant.

On Thursday evening Maria had wandered round the stores in Knightsbridge after college, looking in shop windows, trying to find something to wear, and finally, in a boutique, she had found exactly what she wanted. It was a long, caftan-styled gown, with wide sleeves and a high collar; a blue background, patterned with gold and green. Its simplicity of design was compensated by its colour, and it suited her slightly olive complexion and chestnut hair. She wore little make-up, highlighting only her eyes and her lashes, painting her lips with a colourless lipstick.

It was almost nine o'clock by the time she ventured downstairs to encounter Mrs. Lacey in the hall. The housekeeper looked at her with raised eyebrows and chuckled.

'Well, well,' she said, appraising the gown thoroughly, 'you do look nice.'

Maria bit her lip. 'Do you think it's all right? Not too brilliant or anything?'

'Heavens, no, miss, and at least it doesn't cling to you like a second skin like some of those evening gowns do.'

Maria looked down at the soft folds about her legs and ankles. 'I don't think I would suit anything like that,' she murmured. 'Maybe Miss Griffiths . . .' She stopped and shrugged, and Mrs. Lacey nodded knowingly.

'Oh, no doubt she'll outdo everyone,' she said resignedly, and Maria had to smile.

'You don't like her, do you?'

Mrs. Lacey opened her mouth to reply and then they both became aware that the lounge door had opened and Adam stood on the threshold regarding them. Maria had never seen him in a dinner jacket before, and its darkness accentuated the darkness of his skin, the whiteness of his collar providing a line between. He looked disturbingly attractive, and her colour deepened as his eyes flickered over her.

'Are you ready?' he enquired, his voice cool and expressionless.

Maria glanced round. 'I – I think so. Do I need a coat?'

'I shouldn't imagine so. It's a warm evening. Shall we go?'

He nodded to Mrs. Lacey and stepped forward to open the door, allowing Maria to precede him outside. For all it was a warm evening, Maria shivered involuntarily, and she wondered what it was about Adam that reduced her to a trembling mass of nerves. He opened the Rover and helped her inside, folding her skirt so that it didn't catch in the door. Then he walked round and slid in beside her, lighting a cheroot before starting the engine. He glanced round and reversed expertly out of the drive, swinging the car on to the main road with ease.

Maria concentrated on the road ahead, wondering with a sinking sense of inadequacy whether she had been a fool to agree to come. It was one thing considering the idea in the security of her bedroom, and quite another to carry it out. But she was committed now, and she would just have to make the best of it.

Adam stood on his brakes suddenly as a Mini swung dangerously out in front of them, and Maria grasped her seat to prevent herself from being jerked out of it. Adam uttered some uncomplimentary expletive under his breath and then glanced at her as though the sudden incident with the other car had brought her presence to his mind.

'Tell me,' he said, with deliberate sarcasm, 'do you discuss me with Mrs. Lacey, too?'

Maria's head jerked round. She had been so concerned with her thoughts that that moment in the hall had gone completely out of her mind. But she would not give him the satisfaction of disconcerting her once again, and with considered reluctance, she replied: 'Sometimes.'

Her reply obviously surprised him, for he granted her a swiftly appraising glance before saying: 'No doubt you'll find plenty to talk about after this evening.'

Maria did not reply. She knew he was merely baiting her and she would not give him the satisfaction of knowing he aroused her. Instead, she returned her attention to the passing scenery outside the car, finding the ever-changing panorama more than satisfying. There was something innately appealing about London in the early evening, the streets thronged with sightseers and tourists of every nationality. She wished she knew it well enough to be able to walk about with confidence, and she smiled to herself as she recalled those first couple of days in England and her encounter with the stranger in the park.

Adam sensed her amusement and said: 'Is something funny?' and she sighed, relaxing for a moment.

'I was just remembering that woman who spoke to me in the park,' she said. 'Looking back on it now, it seems much longer than three or four weeks ago.'

Adam's mouth twisted slightly. 'Yes, you were pretty crazy,' he remarked derisively. 'I trust you won't find yourself in social difficulties this evening. You have a talent for making friends with the wrong people!'

Maria felt furious. 'How dare you say such a thing?' she exclaimed angrily. 'Just because I spoke to a woman who seemed harmless enough, you act as though I was in the habit of getting myself into awkward situations!'

'And don't you?' enquired Adam dryly.

Maria turned away. 'I refuse to argue with you. I don't know what's the matter with you anyway. You invited me to accompany you to this party. If I'd known you were going to behave like this, I'd have ordered a taxi. Yours isn't the only transport in London, you know. Perhaps if I'd spoken to Miss Griffiths she would have said I could ask David or Larry as well, and then I could have gone with them. At least they don't bicker all the time!'

From the way his fingers tightened on the wheel, she knew she had got through to him, and the thought gave her some satisfaction. If he hadn't wanted her to come, why had he made such a thing about the invitation in the first place? She was sure he could have persuaded Loren not to send it. He was deliberately destroying what small store of confidence she had, and she wished there was some way she could hurt him as he was hurting her.

The small square where Loren's town house was situated was already flanked with cars when they arrived and Maria's heart sank. While in many ways she was relieved that there was to be a crowd of guests among whose number she could go unnoticed, she also felt a sense of nervous apprehension at having to go into Loren's house and meet so many strange people all at once and probably alone. She was quite sure that Loren would manipulate matters so that Maria and Adam were separated, and despite Adam's condemnation of her assessment of his involvement with the other woman, he himself had said he found their relationship enjoyable and would no doubt prefer any company to that of his stepsister.

Adam managed to park the car in a small mews and they walked together across the square to where Loren's house was a blaze of lights even at this early hour and with daylight outside. The faint strains of music drifted from the upper floor, and Maria wondered whether there was to be dancing, too. She hoped not. Apart from a few modern rhythms, she had no knowledge of ballroom dancing.

Adam looked down at her as they crossed the square, and said: 'Where did you get that dress?'

Maria glanced down in embarrassment. 'At a – at a boutique in Knightsbridge,' she replied half defensively.

'I like it,' he said with decision. 'It suits you.'

His comment was so unexpected that Maria gave him a startled look and encountered his dark gaze. 'I'm glad something pleases you,' she murmured softly, and suddenly he smiled, his teeth very white in the fading light.

'You please me when you refrain from making unnecessary observations about things you don't understand,' he said, cupping her elbow with his hand, his fingers closing round the soft flesh of her upper arm.

His touch caused a quiver of excitement to slide along Maria's spine, and she wondered what he would do if she asked him not to desert her once they got inside Loren's house. With him, she could almost believe she would enjoy herself, but if he should go to Loren . . .

As they entered the hall of Loren's house his hand fell away, however, and a uniformed maid showed her to the ladies' room. Maria did not particularly wish to go to the ladies' room, but she had little choice as Adam turned away to speak to some man he knew and she was left to follow the servant. The hall was filled with guests, all shedding their coats and talking together, and while Adam might feel at home she most certainly did not.

The ladies' room was no better, and after catching a glimpse of herself from a distance in one of the many mirrors that lined the walls she decided she did not want to get any closer. She noticed the jewellery of some of the women, and the way their dresses sparkled as they moved, and glanced rather doubtfully at her own gown. Her hair, too, hung straight and silky to her shoulders, while most of these women wore elaborate hairdos that owed a lot to wigs and hairpieces for effect. Several speculative glances were cast in her direction, but no one spoke to her, and after a moment she opened the door and emerged again into the hall.

For a moment she couldn't see Adam, and her heart almost stopped beating, but then there he was, still talking to the man by the door, and looking wonderfully dear and familiar. She pushed her way through to him, catching his hand to attract his attention, and was surprised when his fingers closed over hers, and he drew her close to his side. He looked down at her with lazy eyes, and said: 'Where did you go?' in a warm, intimate tone.

Maria managed a faint smile. 'The ladies' room,' she replied. 'The maid practically marshalled me there. What do we do now?'

Adam looked at the man he was with and said: 'This is my stepsister, Louis. Maria, this is Louis Markham, one of Fleet Street's better known columnists.'

Maria smiled, and allowed Louis Markham to shake her hand, and then by mutual consent they all moved across the hall to the staircase.

Maria looked about her with undisguised interest. This was the first opportunity she had had to take in her surroundings and now she noted the cream tapestry-covered walls and the intricate delicacy of the chandelier that lighted their way upstairs. A soft blue carpet absorbed the sound of footsteps and a balustrade of white wrought iron was ornately gilded with leaf motifs. At the top of the flight of stairs a landing had been widened and arched doorways led into a long room that had obviously once been several smaller rooms. Here the carpet changed dramatically to deep purple, and the low couches and armchairs that were set about were all made of moccasin-soft white leather. The room seemed full of people, all moving about and talking and taking drinks from the trays held by a dozen waiters who passed amongst them. There was an aroma of perfume and tobacco and alcohol, while an appetizing smell of good food pervaded everything else. It was slightly overwhelming to someone who had never attended such a function, and Maria hesitated on the threshold nervously.

'Come and meet your hostess,' Adam murmured in her ear, and Maria took a deep breath. Any minute now Adam was going to revert to the sardonic, sometimes sarcastic man who tormented her so mercilessly, but for the moment he was treating her as an equal, and it was a bitter-sweet experience.

They left Louis Markham and made their way through the throng to where a crowd of people surrounded the woman who was lounging smilingly on a low couch. The buzz of conversation went over Maria's head as she followed Adam, and a film of perspiration dewed her brow.

Loren saw Adam almost as soon as he approached her devout circle of friends, and she slid off the couch, disturbing the two men who had been talking and laughing beside her, and made her way purposefully to Adam's side. 'Darling!' she exclaimed. 'I thought you said you'd be early. It's almost nine-thirty.'

Adam gave a faint smile as her lacquered fingernails

smoothed the sleeve of his jacket possessively. 'And isn't that early?' he countered lazily. 'I always thought theatre people preferred the night life.'

Loren chuckled, showing her perfectly small teeth. 'Oh, we do, darling, but right now I have to be at the studios every morning at seven a.m. and our hours together slip away too fast.' She pouted prettily, and Maria forced herself to look elsewhere than at those hands that clung so jealously to her stepbrother.

As though remembering Maria's presence, Adam glanced round and caught her wrist, drawing her forward even though she would have resisted. 'You haven't forgotten your other guest, have you, Loren?' he asked softly. 'Don't you think she looks very attractive this evening?'

Maria could have slapped him, she so hated his patronizing tone, and her cheeks burned angrily. It was as though as soon as he was in Loren's presence he changed back to the slightly ruthless man she was becoming so used to.

Loren herself surveyed Maria appraisingly, while Maria allowed herself to acknowledge that Loren really did eclipse every other woman who was here this evening. In a clinging black gown of some satiny material that moulded the girlish contours of her small body she looked incredibly beautiful, and tonight she had dressed her hair in a Grecian style that allowed two long ringlets to fall on to her shoulders like loops of pure gold.

Now she turned to Maria with condescension and said: 'What a pity there aren't any young people here for you to talk to, Maria. But I'm afraid I find young things rather boring in the main.' Her faint smile dispelled most of the malice from this remark, and Maria chose not to be offended.

'I'm sure I shall enjoy myself just the same, Miss Griffiths,' she responded politely. 'I was just admiring your home. I didn't imagine it was so big from outside.'

Loren looked complacent. 'Yes, it is rather pleasant, isn't it?' She smiled again. 'A firm of interior decorators did it over for me a couple of months ago.'

Maria bit her lip. Their conversation was stilted, to say the least, and she was aware that Adam was watching and listening with evident amusement which annoyed her more. Now Loren began to look bored and turned back to Adam appealingly, her eyes seeking his in an intimate exchange of glances.

'I told you, Adam,' she murmured huskily, tapping his chin with her forefinger, causing Maria intense embarrassment. 'I told you Maria would feel – well, out of her depth here.'

Maria's head jerked round and her gaze encountered Adam's. So he had been instrumental in obtaining an invitation for her! She might have known that Loren Griffiths would never agree to invite her without being compelled to do so. Feeling sick with mortification, she turned away, moving purposefully through the chattering groups of people to the comparative seclusion of the arched entrance.

Everyone seemed to be with someone and the waiters who milled about her with their loaded trays eyed her rather curiously, sensing that she was not one of Loren's usual guests. Maria stood striving for composure. She longed to turn and run down that beautiful staircase to the front entrance and escape, but to do so would be an admittance of her own immaturity, so instead she stood where she was, praying for deliverance.

'Good evening, Maria. It is Maria, isn't it?'

Maria's head lifted reluctantly, and then a faint colour invaded her unnaturally pale cheeks. 'Why – why, Mr. Hallam!' she exclaimed. It was David's father.

Victor Hallam regarded her kindly. 'Don't say it,' he said smilingly. 'You're wondering what the hell I'm doing here among all these talented people.'

Maria relaxed a little. 'Well, I am surprised,' she confessed.

Victor nodded. 'That's natural enough. I don't usually attend these sort of functions, but I'm Loren's solicitor, and from time to time I feel obliged to accept her invitations.'

'Oh, I see.' Maria's mouth lifted slightly at the corners. 'I thought perhaps you had a hidden interest in writing or something.'

'Oh, no.' Victor shook his head. 'I'm not at all artistically minded, I'm afraid. Which is a terrible admittance when I'm Loren's solicitor. But then I never like to mix work with pleasure. But tell me, what are you doing here? Did Adam bring you?'

Maria stiffened slightly. 'Yes – yes, he brought me. I – I was with him up until a few moments ago.'

Victor looked round. 'And now he's been annexed by Loren, I suppose.' He nodded knowledgeably. 'I wonder when she'll stop play-acting and get around to marrying him. She wants him badly enough, I'm surprised she doesn't realize the risks she's running in waiting so long.'

Maria swallowed hard. 'Do you think it will be soon?'

Victor shrugged, helping himself to two champagne

cocktails from a passing tray and handing one to Maria. 'Who can tell? If she could persuade him to give up his Islington practice and take a partnership in one of those sleek West End clinics it could happen next week. But somehow I can't see Adam abandoning his ideals just like that.'

Maria sipped her cocktail reflectively. 'You've known Adam a long time, haven't you?'

'Yes, we knew the family when Adam's father was alive. And Adam always wanted to be a doctor. Even when he was quite a young boy. He took a degree in medicine and another in surgery at Cambridge, and we all expected him to become a surgeon. He had the temperament, you know. But then this friend of his died of leukaemia, and after that he decided he wanted to enter general practice.'

'I see,' Maria said interestedly. 'I wonder what made him decide that.'

Victor frowned. 'I think it brought it home to him pretty clearly that not all illness can be cured by surgery. And the better the general practitioner, the better service he can give to his patients. In any event, Adam's an idealist, like I said, and he does everything he can to help the under-privileged.'

Maria nodded, running her forefinger round the rim of her glass. 'But he does have some private patients, doesn't he?'

'Oh, a few, yes. My own family included. But they're a very small part of his work.' Victor regarded her smilingly. 'They have to be. He doesn't have a lot of time to spare.'

Maria finished her drink and Victor turned to pass her another. She took it reluctantly, aware that the heady intoxicant was stronger than anything she was used to. But she felt better with a glass in her hand, although she refused the cigarette Victor offered.

'David tells me you're going to train as a secretary,' remarked Victor suddenly. 'Your good example seems to have had a favourable influence upon my son. He's already suggested starting in the business a month sooner than he intended.'

Maria gave a soft laugh. 'You can't be serious.'

'Oh, but I am. David was like the rest of that crowd he plays around with – lazy and indolent; you set him on his heels.'

Maria hesitated and then she said: 'I suppose you know the Hadleys, too – Larry's parents.'

Victor's expression darkened. 'Yes, I know the Hadleys. I also know Larry. Why? Has he been angling for attention too?'

Maria coloured. 'Well, actually, I did go out with him a couple of times. But Adam seems not to like him.'

'With good reason!' exclaimed her companion heavily.

Maria stared at him, for the moment absorbed in what he was saying. 'Why?'

Victor shook his head. 'It's nothing to do with me,' he replied grimly. Then he studied her disturbed face and sighed. 'Perhaps you ought to know, at that, if he's showing an interest in you.' He swallowed half his champagne cocktail and looked broodingly into the glass. 'There was a girl – you know the sort of situation, I don't need to go into details, and Larry approached Adam for help.' He uttered an expletive. 'Of course, he didn't dare to approach his own father, but Adam was young . . .' He shrugged. 'That's about it. Adam wouldn't touch it, naturally, and I heard the girl had the baby and the Hadleys arranged for its adoption.'

Maria's face was scarlet. 'I see,' she said unsteadily. 'I had no idea . . .'

'How could you have? The Hadleys are a decent couple, and we couldn't completely ostracize Larry for what he had done. Gradually, he's insinuated himself back into the circle, but all the girls are aware of what happened and therefore tread cautiously.'

Maria nodded, recalling with brilliant clarity the way she had stormed at Adam for criticizing her relationship with Larry. He had only been thinking of her, after all, and she felt justifiably ashamed.

She looked across the room suddenly, searching for him, wondering whether he had forgotten her existence by now. Victor lit another cigarette, and Maria said: 'Isn't your wife here, Mr. Hallam?'

Victor shook his head. 'No. She has a headache, or at least that's her excuse. She's not enamoured by your stepbrother's girl-friend, I'm afraid. Not many women are. Loren tends to overshadow them, physically, at least.'

'I know.' Maria sounded wistful.

Victor stared at her quizzically. 'You don't envy her, do you?'

'Not exactly. But she is beautiful, isn't she?'

'Of course she is. But not all beautiful things have warmth and depth. I shouldn't have thought you'd have anything to worry about, young Maria. Your youth and the unwrinkled smoothness of your skin are worth any amount of cultivated perfection. In ten years Loren will begin to look her age, and then watch out.'

Maria chuckled, and Victor patted her shoulder conspiratorially. Then she became aware that someone else was approaching them, his face dark and intense. It was Adam, and immediately Maria's smile disappeared. Victor, however, showed no such inhibitions, and turning as the other man reached them, said:

'I ought to thank you, Adam. This is the first time I've actually enjoyed one of these affairs, and it's all due to your stepsister here.'

Adam raised his eyebrows indifferently. 'Thank you for looking after her, Victor,' he said. 'I've been trying to find her for some few minutes.'

Maria finished the champagne in her glass and Victor took it from her and placed it on a side table. 'We've been having a nice confidential conversation,' he remarked lazily. 'And helping ourselves to some of Loren's excellent champagne in the process. Where is that good lady, by the way? I thought she'd be with you.'

Adam's expression was enigmatic. 'I imagine she's over there somewhere. Someone was prevailing upon her to sing, but I doubt whether her voice will rise to the occasion.' He looked deliberately at Maria. 'I'm pleased that you've managed to take care of yourself so well.'

'Mr. Hallam has taken care of me,' replied Maria coolly, more coolly than she felt. 'Don't let me keep you from your – your fiancée.' The way she said what she did was challenging enough, and even Victor raised his eyebrows with elaborate display.

'I think Maria finds the atmosphere a little overwhelming, as I do,' he drawled. 'And if you want to go back to your hostess, we're perfectly all right. I can even take Maria home later on if you like.'

Adam looked as though he was controlling his features as they tautened considerably. 'Thank you, but I shall take Maria home when it's necessary,' he replied, in a tone that brooked no argument. 'Now, if you'll excuse Maria I'll take her for some supper.'

Maria glanced rather desperately at Victor. The last thing she wanted was to be separated from the one person she could talk to in all this mass of humanity, and any minute now Loren would reappear and demand Adam's undivided attention and then she would be lost again.

'If you don't mind, I'd rather go to supper with Mr. Hallam, Adam,' she said quickly. 'I – I'm sure Miss Griffiths won't be engaged for long, and then she'll come looking for you. I'm quite all right, and you have no need to feel responsible for me.'

Adam looked furiously at her, his eyes blazing with suppressed anger. 'Maria—' he began, in a commanding tone, when Victor stepped forward.

'Really, Adam, Maria's right, you know. We're both in the same boat, in that we don't have a partner. I shall be quite happy to look after her, and then you'll feel completely free to attend to your other duties.'

There was a moment's pregnant silence when Maria felt certain Adam was about to make some scathing comment, and then with obvious control, he said: 'All right, Victor. I'll accept your offer.' He looked at Maria icily. 'However, I will take Maria home myself, is that understood?'

'If you insist,' Victor smiled, and nodded. 'You've no idea how relieved you've made me feel. I shan't have to make conversation with some soulless female whose only attributes are her vital statistics.'

Adam did not smile, however, and with a bleak nod in Maria's direction he walked away, and a few minutes later Maria saw Loren twine herself about him.

Bending her head, she tried to concentrate on what Victor was saying, but somehow it was impossible when the sight of those two together caused an agonizing ache in her stomach. She half-wished she had allowed Adam his way, and gone into the supper room with him. He had seemed to want to take her, and maybe she was being unkind in treating him so coldly, but she also knew that to attempt to analyse her feelings for him in this moment would amount to admitting that the longer she stayed in England, living in Adam's house, the more emotionally involved with him she became ...

CHAPTER NINE

IT was about eleven when Adam sought Maria out. By now she was feeling distinctly drowsy, not only with the heat and the lack of air, but also with the unaccustomed amount of champagne she had drunk. Supper had been served earlier on, and although there had been a vast array of delectable foods to choose from, Maria had not felt particularly hungry. After supper, they had all been entertained by a group of Spanish musicians accompanied by a Spanish dancer whose rhythmic foot-tapping had mesmerized his audience. There had been more wine and more conversation; Maria and Victor Hallam had been joined by Louis Markham and his companion, a rather pretty girl with curly blonde hair, and then Loren had been prevailed upon to sing. Although she had smilingly protested, she had eventually agreed, and while her voice was not spectacular it was quite pleasant to listen to. She sang a haunting gipsy love song, accompanied by two guitarists from the group of musicians who had entertained them. Her performance had been loudly applauded, and Maria could only assume that her audience were ardent admirers of anything she attempted.

Afterwards there was dancing to music from a radiogram, but Victor did not suggest that they should dance, and Maria was relieved. She was quite content to allow the evening to drift over her, and while she still longed to leave, at least by staying she was not in Adam's way.

When Adam did come to find her, she was seated on a couch in the corner, listening rather absently to Victor and Louis discussing the merits of a different kind of court procedure. Both men rose as Adam came to stand beside them, and Victor stretched lazily.

'Have you come to deprive me of my partner?' he enquired reproachfully. 'It's early yet.'

Adam raised his dark eyebrows. 'Late enough,' he commented dryly, and looked down at Maria pointedly. 'Are you ready to go?'

Maria got up as well, swaying a little in the airless atmosphere, and Adam caught her wrist impatiently. 'Yes, I'm ready,' she said huskily. 'Where's Miss Griffiths? I should thank her for a lovely party.'

Adam's eyes darkened. 'That won't be necessary, Maria,' he said abruptly. 'Goodnight, Victor, Louis.'

Maria smiled at the two men, and then before she could say anything more Adam began to stride away, still holding her wrist, and she had perforce to go with him.

They caused many raised eyebrows as Adam stalked past the other guests with a purposeful expression on his dark features, and Maria wondered with nervous hysteria why he was behaving so boorishly. Did he object to leaving so early? Did he wish he had allowed Victor to take her home after all?

Downstairs, an immaculately dressed butler opened the door for them, wishing them a polite 'Goodnight, sir, madam!' but Adam scarcely answered him, merely nodding and propelling Maria before him out of the door.

Outside, the night air was chill and refreshing, but it was almost too much for Maria, and she grasped weakly at the iron railing at the top of the flight of steps which led down to the street, swaying dizzily. Adam halted, and swung round as she pulled out of his grasp, and stared at her with eyes that seemed very black in the subdued street lighting.

'For God's sake, Maria,' he swore angrily, 'how much have you drunk this evening?'

Maria felt slightly sick, and she put a hand to her damp forehead, endeavouring to keep her balance. 'Oh, don't, please, Adam,' she whispered shakily. 'I – I just feel a bit funny, that's all.'

Adam compressed his lips silently, and taking her arm in his fingers, urged her away from the railings and down the steps. With his support, they crossed the wide square and entered the mews where his car was parked. It was very dark and she almost stumbled, but Adam seemed surefooted enough, and presently he was opening the car door and putting her inside with all the gentleness he normally reserved for his patients. Then he walked round and slid in beside her, switching on the engine still without speaking.

They drove out of the mews and into the square, and as they turned towards Kensington Maria felt obliged to say something. Glancing nervously at him, she said: 'Are – are you mad with me, Adam?'

Adam flicked a glance in her direction, his long fingers tightening on the steering wheel. 'Why should you think that?' he enquired, with a degree of sarcasm. 'For pity's sake, Maria, what do you think I am?'

Maria's fingers tightened tortuously round her evening bag. 'I don't know what you mean,' she said uncomfortably.

Adam uttered an expletive and jarred one of his gears which caused him to swear violently under his breath. 'You should know what I mean,' he said force-fully. 'Has no one ever explained the effects of alcohol to you?'

Maria sighed. 'Of course they have. I'm not drunk, if that's what you're implying.'

Adam gave a derisive exclamation. 'Then you're giving a pretty good imitation of being so,' he snapped. 'There are more ways of being intoxicated than you imagine. Just because you're capable of articulating coherently it doesn't mean you're immune from other effects.'

Maria's cheeks burned. 'You love to humiliate me, don't you?'

Adam gave her an impatient stare. 'If I did, I would have allowed you to stay there another couple of hours, by which time you would have been incapable of reaching the door unassisted!'

'That's not true!' Maria was horrified, and for the rest of the journey she remained silent, hating him for his cruelty.

They reached Virginia Grove and Adam drove smoothly up the drive, halting the car in its usual position. Maria fumbled with the door catch and slid out, but again the night air was a little too much for her and she had to strive to reach the front door without mishap.

Adam came after her, reaching past her to insert his key in the lock, and pushed the door open so that she could precede him into the hall. All was in darkness, and Maria guessed that Mrs. Lacey was in bed. After all, it was quite late, and the housekeeper would have no idea what time they were expected back.

Maria made for the stairs, but Adam's voice halted her.

'Don't you think you'd better have some coffee, or you'll have a blinding headache in the morning?'

Maria turned, holding on to the banister rail. 'Thank you, I'm perfectly all right.'

Adam shrugged bleakly. 'As you wish,' he said.

Maria hesitated. She would have loved some coffee, but right now she could face no more of Adam's sarcasm, and she began to make her way upstairs. She heard the kitchen door bang behind him as she reached the landing, and a weak feeling assailed her. She wanted to turn and go back downstairs and be with Adam, whatever he might say to her. She had little pride where he was concerned, she was discovering, and only self-will prevented her from making a complete fool of herself. Were all women like this, doomed to love men even when they spurned and humiliated them? To *love* men . . . Maria pressed a hand to her mouth, and made her way into her bedroom.

The room swam dizzily as she bent to switch on the bedside lamp, and she waited unsteadily until it subsided before attempting to get undressed. Perhaps she should have had some coffee after all. At least it would have had the effect of steadying her system, which seemed off balance at the moment.

She unzipped her dress, and stepped out of it, then threw it carelessly on the end of the bed. Then she went to the dressing table, and lifting her brush began to brush her hair. The task was in itself calming, and after a few moments she felt better. But as she put down the brush, a huge moth flew at her from its resting place beside her perfume, and with a startled gasp she got up and tried to evade it. Her jerky action sent the dressing table stool tumbling over and it landed with a thud that seemed to echo round the quiet house.

The moth sought the windows, and with tentative fingers Maria thrust open the casement so that it could escape. Then she closed the window again, and leant against it weakly, her eyes closed.

Suddenly her door opened and Adam stood on the threshold regarding her with anxious eyes. 'Maria!' he exclaimed, his eyes going to the turned-over stool on the floor. 'Maria, are you all right?'

Maria moved away from the window rather unsteadily, and nodded. 'Yes – I – I'm fine.'

Adam came into the room, righting the stool as he did so. 'Did you fall over this?' he asked, his eyes intent.

Maria became conscious of the scarcity of her attire and put a protective hand across her throat. 'No – no, of course not,' she denied defensively. 'There – there was a moth. It – it frightened me, that's all.'

Adam regarded her doubtfully, and suddenly she flared at him, her weakness earlier and now this sudden confrontation combining to arouse her defensive mechanism. 'Don't you believe me?' she cried angrily. 'What do you imagine happened? Did you think I'd passed out in a drunken stupor or something?'

Adam came across to her, taking her by the shoulders and staring at her with blazing eyes. 'Be quiet!' he snapped fiercely. 'Do you want to wake Mrs. Lacey?'

Maria pressed her lips together mutinously. 'That would never do, would it?' she taunted him.

Adam's hard fingers tightened painfully on her shoulders. 'It may surprise you to know that I was concerned about you,' he bit out savagely. 'I was afraid you might have hurt yourself.'

Maria's breath came in jerky little gasps. 'And what would you have done if I had?' she asked huskily.

'Tended me yourself with that marvellous bedside manner you reserve for your patients?'

'Maria – I warn you—' Adam's fingers moved restlessly against her flesh. 'You're playing with fire!'

Maria's lower limbs turned to water. 'Am I?' she murmured softly, suddenly aware that the way Adam was looking at her was like no way he had ever looked at her before. 'How?'

'Don't you know?' he demanded hoarsely, then with a groan his hands slid compulsively over her smooth shoulders and down her back, pressing her body close against the hardness of his. Maria's lips parted involuntarily, and his eyes darkened as he lowered his mouth to hers.

There was a moment when he might have drawn back, but her response was such that almost without volition his mouth hardened and the kiss which had begun almost searchingly became intense and passionate. Maria's bare arms slid round his neck, her fingers tangling in his hair as she pressed her body closer against his, arousing a self-recriminatory protest from Adam.

'Maria, this is crazy,' he muttered thickly, his fingers lingering against her flesh when he would have pushed her away, but Maria merely cupped his face in her hands, putting her mouth to his again, and the warmth of her skin destroyed his will to leave her. 'Dear God,' he groaned huskily, 'I want you!' His mouth sought the softness of her throat and shoulders. 'Don't let me do this!' He encircled her throat with one hand. 'You're so – so untouched!'

Almost simultaneously they both became aware that someone was watching them, someone who was standing in the doorway to Maria's bedroom, a hand pressed to her throat, a stunned expression on her face.

At once Adam thrust Maria away from him, and his expression mirrored his astonishment. 'Mother!' he exclaimed disbelievingly.

'Geraldine!' Maria's faint ejaculation almost went unheard, but she stared at Adam's mother incredulously.

Geraldine Sheridan regarded them both for a long moment, and then she said: 'Maria, my child, it's very late, and I'm sure you're tired. Go to bed. We can talk in the morning.'

Her eyes flickered to her son, who was raking a hand through his ruffled hair to smooth it into order. As she watched, he pulled off his loosened bow tie, and fastened the button of his dinner jacket.

'Adam,' she said coldly, 'will you come to my room? We have to talk.'

Adam took a deep breath. 'Anything you have to say, Mother, should be said here and now. I'm not a schoolboy, and nor am I in the habit of entering Maria's bedroom. What you saw was the result of circumstances and a little too much intoxicant on Maria's behalf!' He flexed his shoulder muscles tiredly. 'Why the hell didn't you let me know you were coming, or were your reasons similar to Maria's when she arrived so unexpectedly?'

'Adam!' Geraldine's voice was chill. 'I want to talk to you.'

'Well, I don't feel like talking right now, Mother,' muttered Adam heavily. He glanced at Maria, and his expression was veiled.

Geraldine gathered the folds of her housecoat about her. 'Let us at least leave Maria to get to bed,' she suggested bleakly, and swept regally out of the room.

Adam hesitated only a moment, his gaze going to Maria almost compulsively. 'Are you all right?' he asked softly, and her cheeks turned pink.

'Are you?' she countered huskily, and Adam allowed his gaze to linger on her mouth so that she almost felt he had touched her.

'No,' he answered tautly. 'I should never have begun something so disastrous.' He walked to the door, and then looked back at her. 'Should I apologize?'

Maria turned away now. 'No – oh, no!' she exclaimed, shivering, and she heard him close the door quietly behind him.

In the morning Maria felt dreadful. Apart from the fact that she had slept badly, her head ached abominably as Adam had said it would, and she dreaded facing Geraldine and the inevitable questions which would follow.

It was after ten before she roused herself sufficiently to go downstairs, and she knew Adam would have left for morning surgery hours before. Dressed in denim jeans and a ribbed sweater, she felt depressed and apprehensive, and not at all ready to face the day.

She found her stepmother in the lounge, reading the morning newspapers, and she looked up smilingly as Maria came in. 'Oh, you're awake at last,' she said. 'I'll go and tell Mrs. Lacey we'll have some coffee. Do you want anything to eat?'

Maria shuddered. 'No, thanks, but I can tell Mrs. Lacey—'

'You don't look fit to do anything,' responded Geraldine dryly, and Maria subsided on to the couch as her stepmother disappeared to the kitchen.

She came back a few minutes later carrying a tray

and placed it on the low table beside her. 'Now,' she said. 'Cream and sugar?'

'Just sugar, please,' replied Maria, and took the cup she was offered gratefully. The hot liquid was steadying, and she slipped a couple of aspirins into her mouth that she had brought down with her to take.

Geraldine poured her own coffee, added cream and sugar, and then lay back comfortably in her chair. 'Now,' she said complacently, 'we can have a little chat.'

Maria sipped her coffee, and smiled, trying to look and sound natural. 'What made you decide to surprise us like this?' she asked.

Geraldine frowned. 'Well,' she said, 'you haven't exactly been a prolific correspondent since you left home, and quite frankly your father was getting quite worried about you. So I said I would come over for a couple of days and see for myself how you and Adam were getting on.'

'I see.' Maria bit her lip. 'I'm sorry about the letters. As you know, I hate writing them.'

Geraldine sighed. 'So it would seem. Anyway, I'm here now, so you can tell me personally what's been going on. Have you started a course? Or are you still looking around?'

'Oh, no, I started a course over two weeks ago.' Maria hesitated. 'I like it very much, and I like England,' she ended lamely.

Geraldine nodded. 'Good. I thought you might. In any event, it's been quite a holiday for you.' She frowned. 'It's a pity you've started a course, of course, but never mind – there's bound to be something similar nearer home.'

Maria frowned. 'Excuse me, Geraldine, but what are

you talking about?'

Geraldine put her cup down on the table very carefully. 'Now, Maria, don't let's fence about this. You know what I'm talking about just as well as I do.'

Maria frowned. 'But I don't.'

'Of course you do. I'm talking about you coming home with me.'

'To Kilcarney?'

'Where else?'

'But I don't want to go home to Kilcarney.' Maria stared at her stepmother bewilderedly. 'Has – has Adam said I must leave?'

Geraldine smoothed the skirt of her dress. 'Adam and I have scarcely spoken on the subject. He refused to discuss what happened last night and this morning he was barely civil. But even so, you can't stay here. Not now.'

Maria swallowed hard. 'Why?'

'Dear heaven, Maria, you're being deliberately obtuse!' At times Geraldine's accent was decidedly like her husband's. 'Would you be living here after what happened last night?'

Maria got to her feet, hiding her hot cheeks with the palms of her hands. 'N— nothing happened last night.'

'No. But that was because I interrupted you.'

Maria took a few jerky breaths. 'No – no, you're wrong. Adam – Adam isn't like that.'

'All men are "like that",' retorted Geraldine impatiently. 'Maria, I'm not saying that what happened last night could or would happen again. Knowing my son as I do, I'm pretty sure he despises himself for allowing his physical impulses to control his mental ones, but that doesn't alter the fact that you're coming

165

to an age when sexual experiences are a temptation. It's only natural, of course, but I should hate anything – well, untoward to happen because of it.'

Maria, who had been pacing the room restlessly, halted suddenly and turned to stare at her stepmother. 'Are – are you implying that what happened was my fault?'

Geraldine sighed. 'Well, my dear, you weren't exactly discouraging him, were you?'

Maria's eyes widened incredulously, and Geraldine sensed she had gone too far. Getting to her feet, she came over to the girl and put an arm about her shoulders. 'Maria,' she began appealingly, 'Adam is an attractive man. I know, I'm his mother. And believe me, you aren't the first woman to be attracted to him—'

Maria shook off Geraldine's hands. 'So now I'm a woman,' she said, controlling herself with difficulty.

Geraldine looked impatient. 'A figure of speech, no more. Listen to me, Maria, you've been living here with Adam, in close contact with him, for almost a month. It's only natural that the proximity—'

Maria's chest heaved. 'Then why did you let me come here?' she demanded. 'It was your idea, after all.'

Geraldine sighed. 'I didn't imagine anything like this would happen, believe me! I thought Adam was immune from— well, I thought he had more sense!'

Maria turned away. 'Excuse me,' she said. 'I want to go to my room.'

'Now, Maria!' Geraldine made another attempt to put her arm around the girl, but Maria had had enough. Without saying another word she left the room and ran upstairs to her room, flinging herself on the bed with desperate abandon. She had always thought

166

Geraldine was her friend, but now even she had forsaken her. Of course, her natural sympathies were with her son, but even so . . .

She lay there in deep dejection for almost an hour, and then she got up and washed her face and combed her hair. It was no use giving in to self-pity, and Adam had not asked her to leave yet. Although she feared that was to come. In all honesty, she had to admit that living here with Adam after what had happened the night before would be difficult, to say the least. But maybe they could forget what had happened and go on as before. If Adam was able to do it, so was she. The thought of going back to Ireland, putting hundreds of miles between them, was the more agonizing one. It might be years before she saw him again, if ever.

With determination, she changed her jeans and sweater for an attractive short-skirted dress in pink poplin, and after making up her eyes so that they did not look so shadowed and haunted, she went downstairs again.

Mrs. Lacey was in the kitchen, but Mrs. Sheridan was nowhere about. 'Where's Adam's mother?' she asked of the housekeeper, and Mrs. Lacey turned to look at her.

'She's gone to do some shopping, or so she said,' she replied. 'You look dejected. What's the matter?'

Maria sighed. 'Oh, nothing much. Look, do you know when Adam will be back?'

Mrs. Lacey frowned. 'To lunch, I suppose. I haven't heard anything to the contrary.'

Maria nodded. 'Well, I'm going out for an hour. It's only eleven-thirty. I need some air. I have a ghastly headache.'

Mrs. Lacey smiled understandingly. 'The party,' she

observed dryly.

Maria managed a smile. 'Yes, that's right,' she said.

Outside, the sky was cloudy and overcast, but it was still very warm, and she walked quickly down Virginia Grove in case Geraldine should be returning and she met her. But as she reached the bottom of the cul-de-sac, a huge chauffeur-driven limousine turned the corner, and she recognized Loren Griffiths in the back. With a feeling akin to panic, Maria suddenly wanted to run, but Loren had seen her and she leant forward and instructed her driver to stop, opening the window to speak to the girl.

'Good morning, Maria,' she said. 'How opportune. I was just coming to see you.'

'To see me?' Maria was incredulous. 'Why do you want to see me?'

'Get in, and I'll tell you. Smithers can take us for a drive. It will be so much nicer than talking indoors on a day like this.'

Maria hesitated. She had no desire to have a *tête-à-tête* with Loren Griffiths, but what could she do? With a sigh, she complied, climbing into the luxurious back seat beside the actress. Loren instructed Smithers to take them on a circular tour of the immediate area, and then closed the glass screen, cutting them off from his hearing.

'Now,' she murmured, as they moved away, 'we're quite alone.'

Maria felt nervous. She sensed that Loren's reasons for speaking to her would not be pleasant ones, and she couldn't imagine what the other woman could have to say.

'Why do you want to speak to me, Miss Griffiths?'

she asked politely. 'After our last conversation at Fincham I shouldn't have thought we have anything to say to one another.'

Loren lit a long American cigarette and inhaled deeply. 'Then that's where you are wrong, Maria,' she intoned smoothly. 'I want to make your position here very clear.'

Maria frowned. 'I don't understand.'

'Oh, I think you do, my dear. As you are aware, Adam and I have been – engaged – for some considerable time.' She studied the glowing tip of her cigarette. 'In the past, whenever Adam has spoken of marriage, I have always demurred – my career, you know. It's difficult for someone in my position to find time for marriage – a honeymoon – the complications that can arise.' She sighed. 'But I must confess, in recent weeks, Adam has become much more persuasive, and circumstances being what they are, last night I accepted him – accepted a date for our wedding, that is.'

Maria felt all the colour draining out of her cheeks. She had known of their relationship, of course, right from the beginning. But to discover that last night he had set a date for their wedding before coming home and making love to her . . . That was almost too much to bear.

Loren studied her expression intently. 'Is something wrong, Maria?' she queried sardonically. 'Hasn't he told you yet?'

Maria swallowed hard, her mouth was dry. 'No,' she said chokingly. 'No, he hasn't.'

Loren sighed again, almost indulgently. 'Well, isn't that just typical of men!' she murmured huskily. 'They pester you and pester you to marry them, and then forget to tell their own sister about it.'

'I'm not his sister!' the words were torn from Maria.

'Well, stepsister, then. It amounts to the same thing.' Loren shrugged her slim shoulders. 'Either way, you can see that it makes things rather difficult for you.' She shook her head. 'Oh, I know Adam won't say anything – how could he? – he'd feel a heel. But you being there . . . Well, surely you can see it's an impossible situation. That's why I wanted to talk to you about it. To explain Adam's position so that you would understand and make – well, other arrangements.'

Maria felt as though every scrap of strength had left her body. She sat as though carved to stone, and every word Loren uttered was like a needle of fire in her numb body. Realizing she was expected to make some comment, she said unsteadily:

'When – when do you hope to – to get married?'

Loren raised her eyebrows. 'Well, that's the point, darling. Adam's all for getting a special licence and doing it as soon as possible.'

Maria looked out of the car's windows. They were passing along the High Street and unless Loren redirected Smithers they would not be back at the foot of the Grove for almost fifteen minutes. Turning to the other woman, she said:

'Adam's mother arrived last night. She wants me to go back with her. I shall.'

Loren's lips curved into a smile. 'Oh, darling, I knew you'd be sensible,' she said triumphantly. 'I'm sure it's for the best.'

Maria looked out of the car's window again. 'Look, would you drop me here? I – I was going to do some shopping anyway. This would be fine.'

Loren raised her eyebrows and for a moment Maria glimpsed a strange expression on her lovely face, and then she leaned forward and slid back the partition, instructing Smithers to stop.

Maria slid out with alacrity before Loren could say anything else and the big car moved majestically away. She stood looking about her rather dazedly for a moment, and then sought the comparative anonymity of a snack bar. Over a cup of coffee she tried to analyse her chaotic thoughts, but all that was uppermost in her mind was that Adam was going to marry Loren, and all the time he had been holding her, caressing her, *kissing* her, he had been aware that in less than a week he would be Loren's husband.

A real feeling of nausea swept over her and she opened her handbag and took out a tissue, blowing her nose in a deliberate attempt to prevent the hot tears that were crowding her eyes. Inside her handbag were all the travel documents she had used to come to England and on impulse she took them out and examined them thoughtfully.

Kilcarney ... Never had it seemed so appealing. Her father was there, her own flesh and blood, and right now there was no one else to whom she could turn.

With determination, she rose from her seat. There was no harm in making inquiries about flights home, was there? She walked out into the street. With that prospect ahead of her she achieved a temporary escape from reality ...

CHAPTER TEN

ADAM parked the car in the drive and walked into the house. It seemed quiet somehow, and he could only assume that the thundery atmosphere outside had somehow pervaded inside as well. Lifting the pad beside the telephone, he scanned it for any calls Mrs. Lacey might have taken and then walked into the lounge. His mother was seated by the window knitting and she looked up at his entrance and gave a smile.

'Hello, Adam,' she said. 'Have you had a good morning?'

Adam regarded her for a moment, and then shrugged. 'Reasonably,' he replied coolly. 'Have you?'

Geraldine sighed. 'I went shopping. Patrick needed some shirts, so I bought him two as a surprise to take home.'

Adam nodded, and glanced round the room. 'Where's Maria?' he asked, deliberately keeping his tone casual.

Geraldine ran her tongue over her lower lip. 'I'm not sure. She went out.'

Adam frowned. 'Didn't you ask where she was going?'

'I was out myself at the time.'

Adam's frown deepened. 'Have you seen her this morning?'

Geraldine coloured slightly. 'Yes, of course. We – er – we had coffee together earlier on.'

'I see.' Adam was clearly not satisfied. He drew out

his case of cheroots and extracting one placed it between his teeth. After it was lit, he strolled to the door. 'I'll have a word with Mrs. Lacey. Maybe she knows where Maria has gone.'

Geraldine sighed rather impatiently. 'Is it important, Adam? She'll be back directly for lunch. Won't you sit down and talk to me?'

Adam halted in the doorway, flexing his shoulder muscles. 'What have we got to talk about?'

Geraldine stared at him angrily. 'You know the answer to that as well as I do.'

'Do I? I presume you mean Maria and what happened last night.'

'Of course I mean Maria. I'm taking her home with me.'

'*No!*' Adam's voice was harsh suddenly. 'No, Mother, you are not taking Maria back to Ireland.'

Geraldine stared at him incredulously. 'What do you mean? Adam, have you taken leave of your senses? Maria can't stay here after – after – what happened last night.'

Adam's eyes darkened. 'Oh, yes, she can. If she wants to stay, she will stay, is that understood?'

'But, Adam—' Geraldine began, only to find herself talking to thin air. He had left the room.

In the kitchen, Mrs. Lacey was just taking a joint of meat out of the oven, and she smiled at her employer as he came in. 'In time for once,' she said impudently, but Adam did not respond as he usually did.

'Do you know where Maria is?' he asked abruptly.

Mrs. Lacey frowned. 'I expect she's down in the High Street, or maybe she went to the park. She said she needed some air; she had a headache.'

Adam compressed his lips. 'I see.' He glanced at his

watch. 'I suppose she'll be back for lunch.'

Mrs. Lacey frowned. 'I should think so. She would have told me if she had intended having lunch out.'

Adam nodded. 'I guess so.' He raked a hand through his hair. 'Did – did anything disturb you last night, Mrs. Lacey?'

Mrs. Lacey looked at him doubtfully. 'I don't think so, Mr. Adam.'

Adam sighed. 'Okay – okay. Thanks. I'll be in the lounge if you need me'.

He walked reluctantly back into the lounge to find his mother pacing the floor rather nervously. He came in and flung himself into an armchair and Geraldine said: 'Can I get you a drink, Adam? Some sherry?'

'Whisky,' said Adam dryly. 'If you have no objections.'

Geraldine poured some whisky into a glass and handed it to him, allowing her eyes to meet his challenging gaze. 'Do you – do you see much of Loren Griffiths these days?'

Adam's eyes narrowed. 'Some – why?'

'Are you going to marry her?'

'No.'

'You're not?' Geraldine was obviously shocked. 'I – I imagined you were.'

'So did I – once,' he remarked, swallowing half his drink. 'But like many men I find I'm arrogant enough to expect chastity from the woman I intend to marry even if I am unchaste myself!' He held his glass up to eye level, studying its contents intently. 'Shall I be more explicit?' His tone was ironic, and Geraldine twisted her hands together unhappily.

'But, Adam—'

'Later, Mother.' Adam rose abruptly to his feet,

finishing his drink with a gulp. 'I think I'll take a shower before lunch.'

Geraldine watched him leave the room unwillingly, and Adam cast a half-mocking backward glance in her direction before mounting the stairs.

They had lunch at one-thirty when it became obvious that Maria was not coming back for it. But neither Adam nor his mother did justice to Mrs. Lacey's delicious roast leg of lamb, and the soufflé that followed almost went untouched. Adam was restless, and after the meal was over his temper had by no means improved.

Geraldine herself was anxious about Maria now. She couldn't help but recall the way the girl had reacted to what she had had to say, and no amount of self-justification could satisfy the small core of doubt inside her. Perhaps she should not have spoken to the girl as she did, but last night, seeing her in Adam's arms, had aroused all her latent maternal emotions, and something akin to pure jealousy had gripped her. She could not accept that Adam was no longer under her domination, and although she was very fond of Maria, seeing them together had hardened her heart.

Adam, watching his mother's expressive face, said suddenly: 'What's on your mind, Mother? Do you know why Maria didn't turn up for lunch after all?'

Geraldine's expression altered. 'How – how could I?'

Adam thrust his hands deep into the pockets of the navy blue pants he was wearing. 'What did you say to her?' he demanded heavily. 'It's becoming pretty obvious that you've said something, so what was it? I want to know.'

'Adam! About last night—'

'Forget last night and get to this morning,' he said harshly. 'What happened?'

Geraldine sighed. 'Nothing. I simply told Maria that she would have to come back to Kilcarney—'

'You did *what*!' Adam's face was thunderous. 'What the hell did you say a thing like that for? What business is it of yours anyway?'

'*Adam!*' Geraldine was horrified. 'Remember who you're speaking to.'

'I'm finding it hard to forget,' he snapped violently. 'Go on. What else did you say?'

'Very little.' Geraldine moved restlessly. 'Adam, I had your best interests – *both* of your best interests at heart. It wouldn't be right for Maria to stay here, not now.'

'Why?' Adam's eyes bored into her.

Geraldine spread her hands. 'Adam, Maria isn't like Loren Griffiths—'

'I know that!' Adam was barely civil.

Geraldine put a hand to her forehead. 'I – I feel rather faint,' she murmured weakly.

Adam strode across to her, putting a hand to her forehead. 'How convenient!' he muttered, taking her wrist between his thumb and forefinger. 'Mother, if you've caused Maria to do anything—'

'Oh, stop it, stop it!' Geraldine sank down wearily on to a low chair. 'I would never have believed you could treat your mother so cruelly!'

Suddenly there was a ring at the doorbell, and Adam left his mother to stride across the hall to open the front door. He stepped back in surprise when he saw Loren on the threshold.

Loren took the opportunity to step inside, and gave him a slightly reproachful smile. 'Darling, I've waited for you coming all day to apologize—'

Adam raked a hand through his hair impatiently. 'Why are you here, Loren? We have nothing to say to one another.'

'Of course we have, darling. Could we—' she looked around, 'could we go somewhere and talk?'

Adam hesitated, and then led the way into his study, a small booklined room that opened from the hall. He closed the door and gently but firmly disentangled himself from her clinging hands as she would have embraced him. Loren's mouth tightened, but she managed to smile a few moments later, and murmured: 'You are a pig, Adam. I don't know why I love you, but I do.'

Adam stood by the window, staring out on to the flat lawn at the front of the house. 'Whatever you have to say, say it and be done with it,' he said shortly.

Loren sighed. 'I – I've come to tell you I'll accept your proposal,' she said.

Adam swung round. 'My *what*!' He stared at her.

Loren coloured a little herself now. 'I'll marry you, Adam. I'll live here. I'll even allow you to carry on with your clinic, if that's what you want.'

Adam's expression was incredulous. 'Loren,' he said heavily, 'I told you last night we're through – finished! Didn't I make myself clear?'

Loren's fingers tightened on her gloves. 'Adam,' she said carefully, 'you don't seem to understand. I'm prepared to do anything you want – if you'll say the word—'

Adam gave her an exasperated look. 'For God's sake, Loren, go now before you say anything else. It's no good. I told you, I don't love you.'

Loren was visibly quivering now. 'Adam, you don't

mean this.'

'I do, I do.' Adam raised his eyes heavenward.

'I won't let you do this to me.' Her lips thinned.

'How are you going to stop me?' Adam was too taut, too tense, to care if he hurt her.

Loren took a deep breath. 'Everyone knows we've been engaged, if not officially, then unofficially, for ages. I – I could sue you—'

Adam gave her a sardonic look. 'Oh, Loren, don't say things like that. You know damn nicely what a pathetic creature that would make you look, and your public just wouldn't stand it.'

Loren compressed her lips bitterly. 'Why are you doing this to me?' she cried. 'I thought you loved me.'

'I thought so, too, once,' he said. 'Look, Loren, I asked you to marry me a dozen times when I was still fascinated enough to want you. But not any more. You waited too long, Loren. I – I've lost interest. Don't you know that familiarity breeds contempt?'

Loren gasped, 'How dare you say such things to me?'

'Because they're true. Loren, don't let's pretend I was the first man you ever loved.'

'But none of the others meant a thing—'

'I'm sorry, Loren, I'm sorry. But it's no good . . .'

'There's someone else, isn't there? I know there is.'

Adam's eyes were narrowed. 'Yes, there's someone else.'

'Who is it? That gauche stepsister of yours?' Loren watched him intently. 'It is her, isn't it? You're infatuated with her.'

'I don't intend to discuss Maria with you,' he said bleakly.

'Why? She's just a woman like any other woman.'
Loren looked scornful. 'I didn't know you went in for
sweet young things, Adam!'

Adam caught her wrist in a painful grasp. 'I warn
you, Loren,' he muttered heavily, 'don't say any more,
or I may forget that you're supposed to be a lady!'

Loren wrenched her wrist away, but she was obviously shaken by his violence. 'Well, anyway,' she said,
reaching for the door handle, 'I doubt whether she'll
want you after what I told her this morning.'

Adam was beside her in a second, his hand pressing
against the door, preventing her from opening it. 'You
saw Maria this morning? Where?'

Loren grimaced at him. 'Wouldn't you like to
know!'

Adam stared down at her piercingly. 'You'd better
tell me, Loren, unless you want another example of
physical violence!'

Loren shrugged, with assumed nonchalance. 'Oh,
very well then. She was leaving here this morning when
I picked her up in the car. I dropped her in the High
Street.'

'At what time?'

Loren shrugged. 'About twelve, I suppose.'

'And what did you tell her?'

Loren shrugged. 'This and that.'

'Loren!' His tone was threatening.

She sighed angrily. 'Oh, nothing much. I told her
you and I were going to be married.'

'My God!' Adam stared at her savagely.

Loren bit her lip. 'Well, I thought we were,' she
protested.

'After last night?' Adam shook his head contemptuously.

'You were mad with me last night. I thought you'd change your mind—'

'Well, as you can see, I haven't.' Adam wrenched open the door. 'Oh, get out of here before I strangle you with my bare hands!'

After Loren had gone, Adam leaned back heavily against the front door, closing his eyes wearily. Where was Maria? Why didn't she come back? Thoughts of that other time she went missing flooded his mind. He remembered the woman in the park and the narrow escape she had had then. Surely she had more sense now than to get involved with anything like that?

He straightened and went back into the lounge where his mother was still sitting. She looked up as he came in and said: 'That was Loren Griffiths, wasn't it? What did she want?'

Adam hesitated and then shrugged. 'She saw Maria this morning – she spoke to her.'

'You're making a great deal of fuss about nothing, if you ask me,' exclaimed Geraldine. 'Heavens, the girl is only a couple of hours overdue. She'll come back, I'm sure of it.'

Adam gave her a penetrating glance. 'She must,' he said flatly.

By seven o'clock Adam was desperate, certain that something must have happened to Maria. He rang round several hospitals in the area, trying to find out whether anyone fitting her description had been admitted, but no one had. Eventually he got in the car and drove away to look for her himself.

Geraldine, left alone, paced the house unhappily. In her way she was worried, too, but some of that anxiety was directed towards her son. It was becoming patently obvious that his reasons for finding Maria were far more personal than those of a stepbrother looking for his stepsister, and the realization shocked her. When she had sent Maria into Adam's household she had never dreamed anything like this might happen, and his attitude towards her since last night had hurt her deeply. She simply could not accept that Adam, her son – her brilliant doctor son – should be infatuated with a girl like Maria, who had not even Loren's startling beauty to commend her. She had not liked Loren, and she certainly had not wanted Adam to marry her, but nor did she want him to create an alliance with a girl who was so evidently unsuitable. And as for marrying her . . .

The ringing of the telephone brought her abruptly down to earth, and she hurried to answer it. Mrs. Lacey had gone to her sister's as she usually did on Saturday evenings.

To Geraldine's surprise and relief, it was Maria.

'Maria!' she exclaimed, trying to keep the censorious quality out of her voice. 'In heaven's name, child, you've had us all worried stiff about you. Where are you? What are you doing?'

Maria seemed to hesitate, and then she said: 'I'm home, Geraldine. In Kilcarney. I'm phoning from there.'

Geraldine pressed a hand to her throat. 'You can't be serious, Maria! How on earth can you be in Kilcarney?'

Maria sighed. 'I left early this afternoon. There was a flight, you see, and I took it. After what – after what you said, I thought it was for the best.' She hesitated a moment, and then went on: 'Is – is Adam there?'

Geraldine gathered herself. 'What? Oh, no. No, he's

not here.' She pressed her lips together tightly. She would not tell Maria how Adam had reacted to her disappearance, she would not tell her he was out looking for her at this minute. She *couldn't*! Maria was back in Ireland now, thank goodness, and that could be the end of it.

Maria sounded disappointed now as she said: 'Oh! Will you tell him where I am and ask him to cancel the course? I – I shan't continue with it after all.'

Geraldine took a deep breath. 'Yes, I'll tell him, Maria.'

'Will you also arrange to send my things home before you come yourself?' Maria's voice was strangely subdued.

Geraldine sighed. 'Of course I will. What did your father say when you arrived so unexpectedly?'

'Oh, you know Daddy. He was just glad to see me back, I guess. Do you want to speak to him?'

'Y – yes. Put him on.'

Patrick Sheridan sounded characteristically abrupt over the telephone, and seemed more concerned with when Geraldine herself was coming home than with Maria's sudden arrival. But Geraldine knew that afterwards, when she was back, he would demand to know the whole story.

After she had replaced the receiver, she gave a deep sigh. It would be easy to arrange about Maria's luggage now she was here, and Adam could cancel the course. Adam ... She took a deep breath. There was only Adam to face now.

He came home about half an hour later, his face drawn and weary, and Geraldine hurried to meet him as he came in at the door.

'Adam,' she exclaimed warmly. 'Wonderful news!

I've just had a call from Maria!'

The drawn expression lifted somewhat and he stared at her intently. 'Where is she?' he asked swiftly.

Geraldine hesitated, and then, seeing the impatience in his eyes, went on: 'She's in Ireland. You'll never guess, but she's gone home, to Kilcarney!'

'What!' Adam looked stunned. 'My God! When did she leave?'

'There was a flight early this afternoon. She decided to take it – on the spur of the moment, so to speak.'

Adam's jaw tightened. 'Did she say why?'

'No, not really. She just said that she thought it was best, and it is best, isn't it, Adam—' Geraldine broke off as she saw her son's expression. 'Adam! What's wrong?'

Adam strode across the hall and up the stairs, halting half-way up to look angrily down at her. 'You're to blame for this, you and that creature who was here this afternoon!'

'Adam! I didn't tell her to go!'

'Not in so many words perhaps,' he muttered grimly, and continued up the stairs.

With a sinking heart, Geraldine followed him. In his bedroom she found him flinging a dark suit on his bed and begin stripping off the casual sweater he was wearing. 'What are you doing?' she exclaimed.

Adam looked at her. 'I'm going to Ireland. To see Maria. To ask her to come back.'

Geraldine was aghast. 'Adam, you can't!'

'Can't I?'

'But why? Why?'

Adam turned away. 'Not now, Mother. Just get out of my way. You can telephone Hadley and ask him to take my calls for the rest of the week-end. Tell him it's a family emergency. Otherwise, don't say anything.'

Geraldine stared at him helplessly. 'Can't I come with you?'

Adam looked at her ironically. 'I think not,' he replied briefly.

Maria was awakened by the sound of someone banging insistently against the front door. She sat perfectly still for a moment, listening, and when the noise began again she leaned over and switched on her bedside light. It was almost one o'clock in the morning, and it was entirely unheard-of that anyone should come knocking at that time of night to a farmhouse miles from anywhere.

She slid out of bed, but her room was at the back and she could not look out of her window to see who it was. But even as she pulled on her old cotton dressing-gown, she heard her father going downstairs. The dogs had begun to bark and she knew he would have to quieten them before anyone would get to sleep again.

Cautiously she opened her bedroom door and stepped out on to the landing, peering down into the dark well of the hall. Her father had put on a lamp, and was on his way to the door, the two labradors at his heels. He unfastened the bolts and pulled the door wide, and the shadowy figure of a man could be seen outside.

'Adam, by God!' she heard her father say, incredulously, and Maria almost fell over the banister rail peering down at them. 'Is your mother with you?'

Adam stepped into the hall as her father stood back to allow him to do so, and she could see the dark sheen of his hair, and the darkness of his suit in the lamplight. 'No, I'm alone,' Adam said, and she heard her father's anxious:

'Is Geraldine all right, then?' and Adam's re-assurance.

'Then what are you doing here, man, at this time of night?' Patrick Sheridan exclaimed. 'It's after one o'clock!'

'I know it. I would have been here sooner, but the taxi I hired from Dublin broke down several miles away and I've had to walk the rest of the way.' Adam glanced round the narrow hall. 'I'm sorry to intrude like this, but I wanted to see Maria.'

Maria's stomach contracted, and a quiver of apprehension trembled along her veins.

Patrick gave an exclamation, and said: 'Well, you'd better bed down for the night, boy. Maria's been asleep these past three hours.'

'I'm not! I'm not asleep, Father!'

Maria couldn't prevent the words that tumbled out of her mouth, and she began to descend the stairs slowly, conscious of her tumbled hair and shabby cotton gown.

Adam looked up at her and his eyes met and held hers in a long look that turned her limbs to water. Then he looked back at her father, who was looking rather annoyed.

'Maria! Get back to bed at once. This is no time to be receiving callers. Adam, you can talk to Maria in the morning.'

'No!' Adam stepped forward quickly. 'Patrick, I've got to talk to her tonight. Please!'

Patrick Sheridan hunched his shoulders. 'Look, Adam, this isn't London. This is Kilcarney, and I don't hold with all these modern ways. Maria's only a girl, after all . . .'

'I'm eighteen, Father.'

'To bed, Maria.' Patrick was stern, and Maria hesitated for a moment on the bottom stair. Then, meeting her father's gaze, she turned and went obediently back upstairs.

Adam raked a hand through his hair and looked at the older man. 'All right,' he said heavily. 'Where do I sleep?'

'Well, there are no beds made up tonight, boy,' replied Patrick. 'But it's a warm night, and you'll take no harm on the sofa in the sitting-room with a blanket to cover you. I'll get one.'

Adam nodded, and turning walked through to the sitting-room which smelled of beeswax and lack of use. He switched on the light and looked at the horsehair sofa. It wouldn't be particularly comfortable, but at least he was here, in Kilcarney, and Maria was just upstairs.

Maria sat on her bed cupping her chin in her hands, and as she heard her father bid Adam good night she quickly turned out her lamp. She didn't want her father coming into her room tonight asking why Adam had come after the questions he had asked earlier. Besides, she didn't even know why Adam had come.

She waited until the house was silent and then she quietly opened her door again and slowly descended the stairs. The dogs were in the hall, but they didn't stir as she passed them, and she turned the handle of the sitting-room door softly and went in.

The room was in darkness except for a small lamp by the sofa which gave only a shadowy light. Adam was stretched out on the sofa, the rug across his waist. He had shed his coat and shirt and his chest was bare and tanned and liberally covered with hairs, she noticed.

As she closed the door, it clicked, and immediately he sat up and swung round. When he saw her, he stared at her incredulously, and said: 'Does your father know you're here?'

'Of course not.' Maria spoke softly. 'I crept down after he'd gone to bed.'

Adam got to his feet, and stared at her intently. 'You shouldn't have come down,' he said, rather huskily. 'If your father finds us together, he'll imagine the worst.'

'Like your mother did – last night?'

Adam lifted his shoulders. 'I suppose so.' He sighed. 'Maria, I want to talk to you about last night, but like your father said, this is no time to do it.'

'Why not?' Maria's eyes darkened and she spread her hands. 'Adam, why have you come here?'

Adam made a helpless gesture. 'To see you.'

Maria bit her lip. 'Why?'

'I – I guess I wanted to explain—'

'About last night?' Maria was abrupt. 'No explanations are necessary. It was like you said – a result of circumstances.' She turned away. 'You had no need to come here to tell me anything. I – I quite understand. You're going to marry Loren and it looked pretty peculiar – me disappearing like this. Well, I'm sorry. I didn't mean to cause trouble—'

He moved, and she felt the heat of his body behind her. 'Shut up!' he said thickly. 'Shut up, or I'll – I'll—'

His hands gripped her shoulders, and then he pulled her back against him, close against the hardness of his body. 'Does this feel as though I've come here just to make explanations?' he groaned passionately. 'Dear God, Maria, don't you know I want you – I need you –

I can't live without you!' And his mouth sought the smoothness of her neck with disturbing intensity.

Maria's whole body seemed suffused with heat, and she twisted round in his arms, sliding her arms round his neck, pressing herself against him. 'Oh, Adam,' she breathed, as he kissed her ears and the curve of her cheek, 'I thought you thought of me as a schoolgirl!'

Adam's mouth found hers, parting her lips with hungry demand. 'I love you,' he murmured against her hair. 'And I can't think of you as a child any longer.'

Then, with lingering reluctance, he put her firmly away from him, saying rather huskily: 'Have you got anything on under that robe?'

Maria coloured prettily, and would have gone back into his arms, but he turned away, and sought his jacket and the case of cheroots in its pocket. After lighting one, he inhaled deeply, and then trailed the fingers of one hand down her flushed cheek.

'Will you come back to England with me?' he asked softly.

Maria wrapped the robe closer about her. 'You're going to marry Loren,' she whispered tortuously, as common sense reasserted itself.

Adam caught her throat and stared at her with burning eyes. 'I am not going to marry Loren,' he muttered thickly. 'Not now – not ever.' His fingers lingered against her soft flesh, sliding beneath the shoulder of her gown and seeking the warmth beneath. 'Maria, don't you understand what I'm trying to say? I love you – it's you I want to marry and no one else.'

Maria's eyes widened tremulously. 'But – but Loren—'

'I know what Loren told you,' said Adam intensely, 'but she was lying. I told her last night that we were through.'

'Oh, Adam!' Maria shook her head and turned away, reluctantly forcing him to release her. 'You don't want to marry me, not someone like me. Your mother wouldn't like it.'

Adam stubbed out his cheroot violently, and forced her back against him again, his hands caressing her waist. 'I choose my wife, not my mother,' he said thickly. 'Dear God, Maria, I wish you were my wife now. I want you so badly.'

Maria relaxed against him, no thought of denial in her mind, and with determination he pushed her away again. 'No,' he said forcefully. 'Not yet. When I make love to you, I want it to be something you'll remember with delight, not an illicit stolen night on a horsehair sofa!'

Maria had to smile, and he touched her mouth gently with his fingers. 'Go to bed,' he said. 'Please. Before my good intentions give out on me.'

Maria's eyes were warm and gentle, and she leaned forward to touch his mouth with her lips. 'All right,' she agreed softly. 'But I shall be up very early in the morning.'

Adam glanced ironically at the sofa. 'I have the feeling I shall be, too,' he said.

Two months later, Maria was again awoken in the middle of the night. This time it was the telephone ringing insistently beside the bed that disturbed her, and she opened her eyes reluctantly to find Adam already leaning over to answer it. He had switched on the lamp, and his skin gleamed very brown in the subdued lighting. Maria moved contentedly under the covers, savouring these moments when she was just awakening and full realization that she was Adam's wife came to her.

It was exactly five weeks since they had departed to Greece on their honeymoon, and one week since they had come back, and this was the first night they had been disturbed.

Turning on her side, she allowed her fingers to move softly against the skin of his back, and he turned to look at her with darkened eyes as he replaced the receiver.

'I've got to go out,' he murmured huskily. 'Mrs. Fenton is in the process of delivering her latest, and she needs a doctor.'

Maria drew him down to her possessively, and felt his immediate response as his mouth sought the creamy curve of her breast.

'Maria, I've got to go,' he murmured reluctantly. 'I won't be long, I promise.'

Maria sighed and released him, her hair a cloud of auburn against the pillow. 'All right,' she said, smiling a little. 'I suppose we've been lucky not to have been disturbed before this. It's almost three-thirty.'

Adam looked at her for a long disturbing moment, and then slid abruptly out of bed, reaching for his clothes. An hour later when he came back, it was getting light, but there were lights in the kitchen and when he went in he found Maria making coffee.

'I thought you'd like some,' she said gently, and he bent to kiss her.

They drank their coffee companionably, and he said: 'You know, this is the first time anyone has ever done this for me.'

Maria wrinkled her nose at him. 'That's how it should be, isn't it? You haven't had a wife before, have you?'

Adam's smile was slow and enveloping. 'No,' he said huskily, getting to his feet and coming across to her. He bent his head to her shoulder, her perfumed skin arousing his need for her. 'Shall we go back to bed?'

Maria peeped at him through her lashes. 'Do you think it's worth it?' she asked mischievously.

Adam swung her bodily up into his arms and carried her across the kitchen to the hall. As they mounted the stairs, he said softly: 'With you – everything is worth-while,' and Maria was content.

Harlequin Presents..

Three of the world's greatest romance authors.
Don't miss any of this new series!

ANNE HAMPSON

- ☐ #1 GATES OF STEEL
- ☐ #2 MASTER OF MOONROCK
- ☐ #7 DEAR STRANGER
- ☐ #10 WAVES OF FIRE
- ☐ #13 A KISS FROM SATAN
- ☐ #16 WINGS OF NIGHT

ANNE MATHER

- ☐ #3 SWEET REVENGE
- ☐ #4 THE PLEASURE & THE PAIN
- ☐ #8 THE SANCHEZ TRADITION
- ☐ #11 WHO RIDES THE TIGER
- ☐ #14 STORM IN A RAIN BARREL
- ☐ #17 LIVING WITH ADAM

VIOLET WINSPEAR

- ☐ #5 DEVIL IN A SILVER ROOM
- ☐ #6 THE HONEY IS BITTER
- ☐ #9 WIFE WITHOUT KISSES
- ☐ #12 DRAGON BAY
- ☐ #15 THE LITTLE NOBODY
- ☐ #18 THE KISSES AND THE WINE

To: HARLEQUIN READER SERVICE, Dept. N 308

M.P.O. Box 707, Niagara Falls, N.Y. 14302

Canadian address: Stratford, Ont., Canada

☐ Please send me the free Harlequin Romance Presents Catalogue.

☐ Please send me the titles checked.

I enclose $＿＿＿＿＿ (No C.O.D.'s). All books are 75c each. To help defray postage and handling cost, please add 25c.

Name ＿＿＿＿＿＿＿＿＿＿＿＿＿＿＿＿＿＿＿＿

Address ＿＿＿＿＿＿＿＿＿＿＿＿＿＿＿＿＿＿＿

City/Town ＿＿＿＿＿＿＿＿＿＿＿＿＿＿＿＿＿＿

State/Prov. ＿＿＿＿＿＿＿＿＿＿＿ Zip ＿＿＿＿＿

N 308 P